Elieshi Lema

Parched Earth

A Love Story

E&D Limited

Dar es Salaam

E & D Limited
P.O.Box 4460
Dar es Salaam

ISBN 9987-622-22-4

Designed by Petras Maridadi Ltd.
Printed and bound by Tanzania Printers Limited, Dar es Salaam
Cover artwork by Christina Stienberg-Mund

Acknowledgements

Hearts sing. And it is these songs that were the bedrock of this writing. The women: My mother, Ndashiwanga Malema, who is a mine of passions. My daughters, Kokuteta and Ankiza, for their trust in the mother and in themselves, always. The men: My son, Mwombeki, who asked, when he was too young to understand, "how come women do all the work?" My friend, Eric for laughter and sharing and thankfully for not believing in packaged time. B, for being.

I thank my readers, Associate Professor of Sociology, C.S.L.Chachage, University of Dar es Salaam, for his critical remarks and sensitive reading. Associate Professor of Comparative Literature, Fawzia Mustafa, Fordham University, New York, who inspite of difficult conditions still found energy and time to read the manuscript. Her questions, points of caution, suggestions and encouragement were invaluable.

PART ONE

The Struggle with the Daemon

...Remember there are many paths, but the only one that matters is the path with heart. Stay true to its lead, and walk its full length.

Joseph Jastrab
Sacred Manhood, Sacred Earth, 1994

CHAPTER 1

I sit in front of the class watching the children hew knowledge from the quarry of my words. Once in a while one of them looks into my eyes, unseeingly, seeking some magical intervention to give answers to the teacher's questions. And all the time my mind is telling itself stories. My stories, your stories. Our stories. Silently, it extracts these stories from the raw matter of living, matter coughed up like lava from the melted core of existence, mine, yours, ours. There is no timeframe to the stories, to their evolution, they are always there, always bubbling up and sinking back into the lava. Looking at children, listening to them, teaching them and having to punish and reward them lift my mind into the circle of dream, again and again, prying, asking questions. Why do they do the things they do? The way they do them? And why do grown people come to do what they do, the way they do them?

We live in a world, my mind says, which is very strange. Always new, always surprising. In this world we are all trying to draw a circle of comfort around ourselves, every one for themselves, rarely, very rarely for the other. The struggle to remain within this circle creates a matrix in which we travel, sometimes blindly, because our consciousness is often colored by the primacy of our own desires, sometimes finding the road, pushed by a fleeting conscience.

Sometimes we get lost in the maze, but always moving, trying to find our way towards that spot, that warm, keenly desired area of absolute comfort. Always searching. It is like a curse!

The image of the spider comes to mind, the way it spins its web from the very inside of its stomach, for itself, and for trapping others into its power and into death, which is life for itself. Death for one, life for another. The spider spins its power web from the secretions of its stomach in order to survive, doesn't it? Does it know that it is not just the fly that can die inside that web, but also one of its own kind or even itself? Life informs life. I should have been a biology teacher, then I could have had the chance to teach these children and myself how to pry into the nature of living things, drawing out their inside for closer examination and thus be cleverer living with and among them. Would that have worked any better for me? Would that have brought me to knowledge about the intricate nature of the human heart?

The other day, remembering how the air at Sokoni Juu Primary School once vibrated with gossip about Martin and I, the possibility of love having pricked a communal vulnerability, I wished to have been just Spirit. I could have moved everywhere, felt and heard everything that was said or felt, including the unvoiced thought processes. Would that have made me wiser? Or would it have been just unbearable burden, knowing all those things! I realize, with the benefit of experience, that being Spirit would be as scary as death. Entering the minds of others at will, silent as light, taking record of their thoughts! No, I think we are all better off guessing, as the pupils did then and still do now, thinking that I know what they are thinking about, especially when they try to lie, that it is the neighboring child who was disruptive, or who took the ruler from my desk, not them. They cannot figure out how I detect the culprit. They are not aware of the trickery of the mind, how it makes them speak their crime through a word, a gesture, or the shine in the eyes. The tender thing about children is their raw cunning, simple, without malice. Theirs is a natural animal instinct for self- preservation and the drive born of greed for the immediate moment's gratification. Yes, I think children live now, this moment. Adults plan for tomorrow, they weave tomorrow's life now, and in that pre-occupation, the gift of life in the present moment eludes them, gone before it is lived. Only the very naïve take the future given in the moment, living it fully. And we laugh at them, wondering why they are not like us, planning, searching for pleasure and comfort. We beat them with our disdain, just like we teachers beat the children because we wrongly judge their actions, the beating being an easy means of establishing power, control, easier than looking for truth, or giving guidance and counseling. I have stopped beating children for anything, including failing tests, coming to school late, making noise, even for fighting each other. They still think I am strict.

Yes, my mind is used to traveling, everywhere, places I have been and have not been, crossing past times and future times, spinning webs like the spider, trying to weave a life which is not a death trap like the spider's. Aunt Mai, long adapted to living in the social web, seemingly not disturbed by the questions it raises would probably tell me, "That is just how things are." I came to learn that she knew so much more than the way things were, but it was her way of telling me that I can not know all things at once, every knowledge has its time. She told me once, " A woman is a social orphan, truly," referring to my mother, but Aunt Mai had proceeded to wear down the silk threads, by doing things that gave the social orphan a parent. I realized, as I talked to her more, that Great Aunt Mai was shrewd but a very loving woman. She became our pillar of strength, for mother and especially for me. She would say, 'that is how things are', but would then undermine, in her own subtle way, that law which made things that way. When I became a teacher and went home with presents for her and uncle Simbo, as well as my mother and all my brothers, she said, "Ah, truly, God's child, you have got a husband now. This job of yours is the *real* husband. Hold on to it like life."

I did not come to this job by choice. Like many other girls, I wanted to go to secondary school, but my grades did not allow. I was among the many girls in our school that got our second choice. "Your grades did not allow you to go further," the teacher had said, simply, cutting off any complaint that had started showing in my eyes. Being a teacher was the only available opportunity, which I took with gratitude to God and felt luckier than my brother Godbless who got no chance at all, having failed his exams. He is still in the village, working on the land. He has never liked it, never forgiven fate for that raw deal. I remember an uncle Godbless had gone to, pleading his case for school, said to him, "Son, we walk the road we were born to walk, truly." Godbless had hated that fatalism, had hated the uncle who pronounced it, as if the man had chosen the road for Godbless. In many ways, Godbless has continuously refused to reconcile himself to the fact that he is a villager. Often, he tries to escape, but the keys perpetually elude him.

He had dreams of becoming a big person in some office doing very important jobs and wearing suits and neckties and talking in a foreign language. That would please him, make him feel realized, put him in a class apart from others. This dream included building himself a big house in town, not the village where he would live with a wife who was equally learned. Even as a young boy, he had an image of the kind of wife he would marry and the children he would have. When as children, my friends and I played mother, Godbless drove a big car he made from the soft pith of a banana plant around the courtyard. The noise of the engine he made told of the road he was traveling, climbing hills in high gear or moving smoothly over flat tarmac. He fashioned a necktie for himself out of a dried piece of banana bast, tied it round his neck and made believe he was a minister, speaking a language he believed to be English. He felt important, even in acting. When he got out of his car, his one hand would be in his shorts pocket, his head held high and his face creased with serious intent. He knew just what he wanted to be. He often talked of giving mother a lot of money, money that he obviously would have, so mother would not have to work so hard and could laugh more. Even when he was in standard four, he already talked of having several degrees. I did not know what he meant then, or who gave him the idea of degrees, but he seemed confident enough to say, "Degrees take a person far, sister." I agreed with him. I always did, because his dream was part of an alternate world he created and which both of us believed in. We talked about our future as a matter of course, because we believed in the story of our future that he had created. It was so real we could touch it. We just had to wait for it to unfold.

My brother Godbless has always felt close to mother. As young children, we had neither the words nor the consciousness to voice the love, but looking back, it was the love that made Godbless declare: "I will buy Mother good clothes and build her a big house and give her lots of money. I will be a big person then." Mother was a part of his dreams, the flag of his success. He would say those words to me, as if appealing for my understanding and complicity, like a promise to which I had to stand witness. He repeated this promise to me when mother was sad or withdrawn, when she would not laugh at all. We all knew then that something would be troubling her heart, because as her children, we survived in her good spirits, became naughty and more playful when she was happy. It is not that we spent time thinking about mother's sadness, we did not know what sadness was. We worried more about the effect of it on us. We did not know much about her struggles with life. What mattered most to us was that we had enough food to eat when we felt hungry. So as Godbless grew older, the dream still with him, albeit fraying and losing color, he continued to think of ways of helping mother by sending his younger brothers to school. He knew by then that he would not have a degree, but at least he would have money.

I did not have a dream. I could not fashion one from my mind and build it up and act it out like Godbless did. My mind had not started telling itself stories yet, had not started weaving dreams like one knits a nicely patterned sweater from wool. All I could imagine was cooking, washing and taking care of my brothers. That did not seem quite like a dream. At least, if it could *be* a dream, it could not match the flamboyancy of being a minister. Cooking and washing did not give me the certainty and elation that Godbless got from his dream, so I believed in his dream instead. When he acted as minister, I wanted to be someone going along *with* the minister. I would try to do things that would include me in the aura, but often that part was mute. It was Godbless who spoke and knew just what to do. He knew how to be authoritative, and in the make believe, he made me obey him. I believed his dream could also be mine, that if he became the minister, *I* would be someone too. He saw far, I was happy that it was so. But as time went by and the dream of becoming a scholar and minister was lost in the fog of poverty and opportunities denied, this desire crusted into something hard and cold that is now detected only by those who know him intimately.

I worked hard as a young girl. Hard work was a practical lesson I internalized just by watching my mother. She was always up by five in the morning and would drag us both out of bed at six. We were hardly able to see anything at such an early hour, we would still be sleepy. We never got used to this daily routine, we always grumbled in a muffled way so she would not hear. She made us do chores before we left for school. We fetched the water she needed for the day from the stream, a kilometer or so away, our feet numb from the cold, early morning dew. Back from the stream, I washed the previous night's dishes and Godbless swept the courtyard. Then we washed ourselves and had porridge before running, barefoot, to school.

Then I grew up, left home and went to a boarding secondary school and later became a teacher. It was initially exhilarating, being on my own, with my own room, doing a job with a salary! It felt so new, for a time. My letters to Godbless, talking about the good life of teacher education, must have crusted his hurt to a stone. That life was *supposed* to be his! He was the man of the house, the male child of the family, the name carrier. But he did not write any of those things in his replies. He talked of the state of coffee crop and the maize in the fields and the coming of the weeding season when they would need money. He imagined that I had become something else, like his dream had shown him. He did not know that even with my learning, I found myself doing most of those things I did as a child. I was already conditioned by the reality of my childhood, and unlike him, did not look for alternative realities that I could recreate and make mine. I still rolled into the mould as naturally as breathing! So I grew vegetables in a small plot, not because I could not buy the produce in the market, but because I had come to love cultivating the earth.

The small garden was made from virgin land that was dry and full of stones and seemed so resistant. Ah, but what kind of earth could defeat me, refuse to yield to my hands? I remember feeling proud when the vegetables thrived. Mother had done her job well.

I started growing all kinds of crops as a small child. When older children initiated younger ones like myself into games and adventurous explorations in the wilderness of life, Mother initiated me into the world of work. As soon as our hands were big enough to hold it, mother gave Godbless and me a hoe, and we cultivated the food we ate. We would work behind her, digging holes for seeds or shaking the earth from the grass so that the farm was clean of weeds and ready for planting. We did not complain. We knew, even as children, who had the privilege of play and who did not. So we learned to enjoy it, because sometimes we turned the work into a game by putting more seeds into the holes, or covering up the grass with soil so that mother would not see, almost bursting with suppressed giggles at our success. Digging, keeping animals- cows, goats, chicken- was part of our life. Caring for people and animals became a habit that would shape my life. As a girl child, my mother would leave me in charge of the house, going out for the whole day. She would simply say, "Doreen, look after the home," and would be gone, often very early in the morning. I would have to organize my brothers, even Godbless who was older, so that Alfred would not be left alone when I went out to cut grass for the cows or fetch water. Later in the day, I would look for something to cook so that my brothers would not starve. I learned to rummage through the farm looking for potatoes and vegetables that grew randomly among the maize, bananas, beans and coffee. In the course of following behind my mother as she worked in the farm, I had learned to identify plants and vegetables that were edible. My mother would sometimes point them out to me, casually, making me harvest them behind her, correcting me if I did the wrong thing.

These practical lessons were given as she weeded or planted or harvested one crop or another. In the basket she brought with her would be an assortment of spinach leaves, sweet and Irish potato leaves, young bean leaves and many others, the names of which I did not know. Always, the farm had something to give. Always. It was not hard for me, therefore, to collect something with which to make a meal for my brothers. It did not matter whether the food tasted good or not. I never thought about the taste, and the boys never complained. If I felt too tired, I made my brothers eat the avocados, the lemons or the bitter tomatoes in the banana grove, whether green or ripe. They seemed to understand that at such times there was no choice. Either they starved or they ate an abundance of fruit in varying states of ripeness but good enough not to hurt their stomach. Sometimes, I would cook enough to put aside some for mother. This was only when there was something like flour or bananas in the house, but often we left nothing for her. She never demanded food when she came back, tired and worn out. We never noticed how hungry she looked. There were times she came back with foodstuffs, a half bunch of bananas or flour, and, very rarely, rice. We rejoiced when she brought rice, which tasted particularly special when she cooked it with beef. It was like a celebration, something not to be forgotten for a long time. The struggle between a woman and the land, the struggle to make it give- a crop, a fruit, any kind of food, was an experience I knew instinctually. Life had given me the knowledge, which as a child, I took in by rote, without question or analysis. When I was old enough for mother to talk to me, she used to tell me that women are most at home with the soil. I did not know why that was so, but looking at her over the years, I think it was because working the land complemented the woman's role of nurturing. Women nurture the earth like they do children and husbands. Loving them is not enough, a woman must also teach, persevere, must nourish spiritually, over and over again. It is the same with the earth. A woman gives her attention to the earth because she knows that barrenness of the land is death for herself and her children. And then again, the earth is so willing to be used, so willing to give, freely, over and over until it is completely exhausted. Perhaps, instinctively, women have come to find the earth a friendly ally in their struggle with life as mothers and wives.

Life taught me something else, that mother was poor. I was grown and going to school when I learned that mother used to go and work on other people's farms for money. A girl in my class revealed this to me after I had badly defeated her in a game. She took defeat badly and in her moment of shame and mine of pride, she remembered something that brightened her mood. She laughed, and said, "I let you win of course, *and you are so poor* you need to win sometimes." She opened her eyes wide as she gesticulated, her whole body shaking, her hands flying in all directions, sticking out her tongue like one about to vomit. She screwed up her mouth just so, in that way that makes the one scorned feel like scum, like a dirty and useless rug.

"You lie, you've lost, you lost the game. I defeated you," I retorted, so angry I was foaming at the mouth. A cold stone of anger had settled in my throat, making my voice hoarse. How could she abuse me like that, saying *I* was poor!? Some voice in me warned me against crying and I swallowed the stone, hot and bitter as it was, stuck out my tongue in turn and scowled even more than she did.

She said with relish, "My mother said your mother is poor and you are also poor. That is why she gave her the sugar and rice yesterday." She spit out the word *poor* as if it was a gooey, rotten mango creeping with worms!

I had no more words for that girl. The abuse she had inflicted on me felt heavier than a boulder! The pride of winning the game went down my throat with pain. Why did she call me poor? What crime had I committed to deserve the insult? I became very careful afterwards, lest I was branded something else as embarrassing as being poor. Even then I was not quite sure what it meant and I was scared stiff of asking anyone. I knew somehow that it was related to having no food, which in my opinion, we always had. So what else did being poor mean? Anyway, it did not feel nice to be known by everybody in school that I was poor, and that my mother worked on other people's farms! Mother had never told us what she did when she was away from home. It never occurred to us that it could be something shameful or that it was related to poverty.

I never told anyone at home about this, not even Godbless. I was afraid he would seek out the girl in school and beat her, then she might call us something else. But from the day of this revelation, I was bonded to my mother in this secret of our life. I worked harder everyday when she was away, knowing that somehow hard work would relieve 'our burden' of being poor. I never forgave or forgot that girl, her face masked by an ugly scowl, her wide- open eyes dancing with victory. She got married to a shopkeeper, had five children and became accordingly fat as required by custom. The long ago bitterness stayed with me like a stain on white cloth, so that even as adults, we could only greet one another with a polite smile.

So as a grown up girl, I did not need to learn. I cultivated the earth and was proud of it. I could always see the garden through the window of my room and it was refreshing for me to know that I had finally tamed that piece of earth and made the vegetables grow. I liked the feel and smell of animal manure on my hands, the softness of the earth, the smell of the soil, especially after the rains, the mystery of growing things. Those smells have a certain intimacy which transport me back to my childhood, evoking the caressing smell of mother's body. When I got tired of looking at pupils' notebooks, I engaged my mind thinking of how to make the garden better, already seeing the possibility of those vegetables blooming right before my eyes! I spent a lot of time looking for manure from those who kept cows or chickens, begging for it as if it was something of great value, watering the plants with water I fetched from the tap in the compound despite the bitter complaints of the landlord. Anyway, I did not use most of what I grew. I gave the produce away to friends and house mates, as I was single and living alone.

Sokoni Juu Primary School is on the southeastern side of the mountain, situated just where the slope tapers into the lowland.

Lowland schools are a little like village schools and a little like town ones. The teachers are cleaner and smarter, dress like townspeople, and act a little like them in that they drink beer, for example, rather than local brew. Women are less reserved in talking with men and there is more socializing among the genders than one sees in rural schools where tradition has locked people in strict ways of life. The sojourn at a teacher training school had helped to clean off my habits a bit, lessening the rural-ness in my behavior so that I blended into the new post without too much effort.

I was assigned to teach geography. I was young, full of energy and enthusiasm. I volunteered to run school projects, planning, organizing and mobilizing teachers to ensure that the projects were successful. That made me happy, working, managing, and thinking only of achievement. I was very anxious to show how good I could be. It also made me popular with the teachers and with the pupils. My headmaster, unaware of my history, always praised me saying, "Doreen is the best and the most hard working teacher this school has ever had." It was not so with the other teachers. They considered me foolish to work for a school as though it were my own! What benefit did I think I would get? But I loved the praise. It was like a present, like winning a prize. Appreciation for doing what I always thought ordinary and expected of me, and for which I had never been praised before. It fuelled the energies within me that twenty - five years of living had not yet exhausted.

CHAPTER 2

Ten years later, having moved only once to another school, I am still teaching geography to standard five through standard seven, still doing the same things, with a little less drive, a little less passion.

At Sokoni Juu, I pushed the pupils to excel and did not entertain flimsy excuses they gave for not doing schoolwork. They spread the reputation among other pupils that I was strict and hard, because I did not see the tears they abundantly shed when they were punished, often by what they hated most, more homework. They made faces behind my back, called me names, but that did not deter me. Assistant headmaster and discipline master, Zima Alfonse, liked the way I pushed the students in my classes to do better and be serious with their lessons. He agreed with me that teachers had to be hard but we differed on the issue of beating.

"Beating can be a motivation for learning," he said. "Sometimes it is the only thing these children understand."

"Human beings have a natural hatred for punishment. It never brings lasting results," I argued.

"People remember when they are hurt, so they protect themselves from being hurt again. That way, one can maintain order," he insisted.

It was no accident that Zima was the discipline master. He was hard, opinionated and a keen observer of rules. The headmaster relied on him to maintain law and order in the school, so differing openly with him was not the thing to do. The other teachers watched with curiosity. They could not argue with him and get away with it. "What can he do, he loves her," they said. But they too found my friendship with Zima an advantage. They used me to raise issues in staff meetings, knowing that the complaints would not be ignored. But even as they gossiped behind my back, they would still come and ask for my help, and because I never harbored a grudge against them, I was always ready to teach on their behalf, always ready to offer a hand when they requested. "You are young Doreen," they would say, "you come and help move these boxes." "You are young Doreen, take my class out for a lesson, my sister, I am not feeling well. Doreen..."

Now I do the same thing that fellow teachers used to do, but with less authority over the younger teachers. Age does not command as much respect in the city as it did in the rural towns, nor are teacher relations the same.

I had inexhaustible energy then. I bounced with it and allowed my colleagues to use it. There was a living daemon inside me constantly pushing for action, for pre-occupation of the mind. This daemon found residence in me when I left home to study teaching. It took the form of a lingering loneliness that accompanied me everywhere I went, like a shadow. It was a quiet presence that seemed to threaten my sanity and sense of peace. I needed to be constantly active, so that I would not think of things that made me sad, so I would not cry. I became afraid of myself, afraid of thinking about myself, about mother and my younger brothers. Why didn't we have a father? How come the father did not want to be the father? Why did my mother not talk to her parents? How did all of them live happily while we lived poorly with our mother? Is this what made my mother so sad sometimes? Why were we a little different from the other families? Why? Why? Why?... Because with the birth of the daemon, the stories started coming, spilling out of me of their own free will. I was afraid of them. I was afraid of looking at the stories. And the daemon knew, this mute presence that breathed fire inside of me, scalding me with desire for its wants, knew I was afraid. So I struggled with it, fighting its power over me, refusing to be made sad by my history. What did it matter if we had a father or not as long as people did not know? And if anyone asked, I could create a whole life the way I liked, projecting what I thought others wanted me to be. Don't we always add on to a desired image as an alternative to what we are? So I allowed the daemon the domain of the inside, the deep down world where people did not see. The outside, the world of people and matter was under my conscious control.

I lived externally, my life ruled from the practical part of the conscious mind. That way, I was more sure of things, I knew just what I should say and do, and how and when. I could laugh then, take things easy. But there were times, when this exterior energy and vibrancy was eclipsed by dark moods, strange even to myself. Why did this happen to me? I would call upon fellow teachers, talking about nothing, helping with chores, but eventually I would be pulled down into myself to face the memories. Then, even the sounds I heard were without vibration, without tenacity, as if they came from loose guitar strings. Such moods opened a void inside me that felt raw and tender and extremely vulnerable. I used to feel like that as a child, especially when I was too tired and did not know why I should be so tired, when I felt that nobody really cared, not even my brother Godbless or mother. I saw myself as a captive without a savior. Sometimes, the raw feeling came when I had hurt myself and I would run to my mother, crying, wanting her to hold and comfort me and she would not be there. The urge would be so great I would seek her out where she was, cutting grass or weeding. I would be crying, my face wet with hurt and tears and she would pick up a stick and threaten me saying, "Stop crying before I thrash you!"

"But my knee is bleeding," I would complain, raising my cry to a shrill wail. I would feel quite helpless with the pain, not the scrape, but the other pain inside me. Then only after seeing how brittle the feeling was would Mother allow herself a minute to look at the hurt. "It is a small thing. Go wash it with salt water."

I would leave, unwillingly, sniveling, hurting.

I never would dare use salt water to clean a scrape, so I left it uncleaned, the rest of the day, looking at it every so often, feeling a wave of self pity come over me. I wilted, because of the unsatisfied urge that hurt like a scald. I never could fill that void with anything, all the way into adulthood.

The memory of this childhood time revisits me every time I see my daughter Milika cry her tearless cries, trying to impress her dislikes on me. I know this one to be different because she has known me as mother. I have walked around with her on my back, I have held her and listened to her when she came to me crying. She has slept in my arms. So I know, her tearless cries are often a game we play. I allow it time, I indulge in it. Milika can manage a five- minute tirade to put my patience to the test. She knows she is testing her resilience against mine, and depending on the ruling mood, either she or I will win. I never had opportunities to play such games with my mother, there was no time, no place for it in our lives. Milika has shown me that mothers and children play love games, that they are a necessary communication between all mothers and their children. Women internalize the skill, it becomes part of their character which the shrewd ones come to use with men, unconsciously, as if it were part of their own nature.

The sharp want for love became a small bubble in the deep inside where the daemon lived. So when I was alone, as in the night, I felt the vacuum, the restlessness and the lack of the inner agitation that lent energy and intensity to the things I did. Such were the times when the living presence stirred in me. It seemed to rise from the inside place, floating in the body, arousing the urge to be held in loving arms and be touched and talked to. It felt like a mute scream for love, a yearning for attention and recognition of the want. As a young woman, I often wondered if it was a longing for a man. But even when I finally had a man and felt loved, it still came, claiming its own existence, its own reality. It was like wanting a flower in bud because the beauty in the bloom was without mystery. I would be alone with the night, sleepless and afraid, fighting a daemon craving for the elusive that was still nameless in my world of dream. Why? I would ask the mute scream, why hunger for the indefinable?

Sometimes, it took to feeding the imagination, creating images to make the alternative desirable, bringing it closer to consciousness where it could be felt. Those were the stories I was so afraid of. I was confused by the reality of my life, and afraid of the stories created by a mischievous, untamable resident daemon. I hungered for a life that was not mine, a life that was not there. I was like a desert traveler running after a mirage, driven by a persistent thirst for water. I felt helpless as the daemon overpowered my mind, searching in a language all its own. My following in this search was silent. I could not resist, as it directed my eyes, ears, my mind and all my body, defying logic and any rational thinking. It was king, my body, its willing slave. And after taking its own time, days, sometimes a whole week, the presence would retire and the yearnings would subside. Something in me would be free again. Life would go on and I would notice things around me more, forget less, my mind would be keen to the physical world.

I had come to label these moods the loneliness trap. Was this what Godbless sometimes felt when he withdrew? Later, he expressed it in a longing for his father, an urge that threatened to suffocate all happiness in his life.

Zima, my friend, became sad in the shadow of these moods, but he brightened in the warmth of my happiness. I was so changeable, so unpredictable in that. He was quick to criticize me saying that I was selfish and full of myself, without regard for others. That must be what I made him feel. He was not shamed to say that I was egotistic, an insensitive woman whose world started and ended at my feet! That, however, did not dampen his love for me. Good - hearted Zima forgave me quickly because when the daemon went undercover, I felt light and energetic. Laughter would bubble up easily, vibrancy thrived in me like a charm. Zima would crave for the vitality he saw. "You make my heart soar, Doreen. There is something so beautiful in you that I wish to be near to, all the time." Could it be that holding my body led his heart into a forest of un-definable quests, so that he said, " I can not help that feeling, I can not control it." And I would look at him with so much compassion my eyes watered.

"Please, try to love me, Doreen. I need you," he would plead. Whatever he felt about me was not the same as I felt about him. But how could I tell him that the exterior happiness I showed did not come from that place where love was found? How could I tell him that the happiness we felt together did not make my spirit fly, floating in the lightness of fantasy to let me distinguish the peculiar magic in bird cries or let my mind move, as in osmosis, into the alternate reality in which art and the power to love grows and thrives into existences larger than life? Was that his definition of what he felt? No matter, I couldn't speak the truth. Zima loved the vulnerability I felt so helplessly. How could I protect him from that?

When some bold teachers teased him about our relationship, he suffered. "Do you like it when people tease me?" he would ask, hurt. "How do you think I feel being teased about it when I don't get anything?"

"But I can not be held responsible for that, Zima surely," I would retort, feeling unfairly blamed. "People will always talk about things they know nothing about."

"You are just stubborn, Doreen. You wait and see, I'll break your stubbornness with my patience." The trust in the power of his feelings was daunting.

He continued to press for marriage, trying to convince me that we were perfect partners, that we would be happy together because he would live his life towards securing the happiness of his home. He implored me to think of how happy we would be with our children. "*Our* children, Doreen! Can you not see?"

I could not see, because my inside remained quiet to his request, without any stir, and my body felt nothing.

Then, one day, Martin came into my life.

CHAPTER 3

I attribute some moments of illumination about certain aspects of my life to age and maturity. I no longer agitate, getting worked up by issues outside my power to change. I have now largely, though not completely, accepted that fate will invariably carve out the route my life will take. Now I can say that I, like any human being, am like a speck in the whorl of the God force which rules life. We depend on the indulgence of the God force in order to make any impact on our lives, which again is dependent on the power of our Spirit, how keen the desire is to do what we say we want to do in life, how clear, urgent and immediate the need is to our life. But the common, the banal, the embodiments of great appetites which feed into our life of matter surrounds us like the thin translucent sheath marking the immediate boundary of fetus space within the mother's womb. Often, because of this sheath shrouding our mind's eye, we never see the magic when it comes. We are always, as we live the every day life, on the threshold of truth. Always on the threshold of knowing love, or magic or God, because magic lives in the midst of our life. We take too long to see it, and sometimes do not see it at all. I lived all my childhood and youth looking for magic, wanting it, craving it. Did these moments come and pass me by? Did the preoccupation, of Mother and I, to feeding bodies, deny me, as a girl child, the privilege to feel things of beauty around our life? Was the craving already an accepted state of consciousness? I didn't know anything except what was plainly obvious. I couldn't have known, although I felt the need. When Martin came into my life and offered love, he found the doors open and walked in. He filled the emptiness with his words, his wants, moods and laughter. My body, which had known mostly work and was accustomed only to being fed, washed and bruised, came to know the feel of Martin's hands, his mouth, and yes, the intimations of his penis. I have never been able to push him out of that space. Not even the coming of Joseph, the man who took away the weight of despair that had threatened to kill my spirit after Martin's abandonment, much, much later in our married life, could push Martin from the space in the very core of my soul. I just moved him a little off center, so that Joseph could find his small space in my heart and I could continue to live.

Martin came into my life as if by force of fate. Again, at school the Headmaster had said, "Doreen, go to the seminar of geography teachers in Arusha. The senior teacher cannot afford the fare." And so I had gone instead of the senior teacher, arriving late and going straight to get my allowances. An official had come from the ministry to do just that and had it not been for the cancellation of flights, I would have missed the money for a week. I found him frustrated at not being able to fly back to Dar es Salaam and I was impatient to get my funds so I could plan my shopping in time. I had figured it all out, what I would spend on myself, what I would save to send mother and if possible, a little for Godbless too.

When I went to see the accountant at the hotel room turned

office, he was idly reading a newspaper. He looked up, brightened up a bit and said, smiling, "I thought beautiful girls like you would know how to be punctual. I could have left this morning for Dar."

"Good," I said.

"Good what," he asked.

"Good you didn't leave," I said.

He stared hard at me for seconds, most likely judging my rashness, counted out the money and handed it to me. I left with a hurried "thanks." I felt happy that my plans would be fulfilled. All I needed to do was to organize, with the other women, about when and where to shop. Something at the back of my mind lingered over the strange familiarity I had felt with a man I knew nothing about. It was a fleeting thought that stole into my conscious mind for less than a minute and was gone. Afterwards, I participated fully in the seminar. I knew I would have to submit a report that must please the Headmaster, since letting myself down was not something I was ready to do. I was already an example among teachers and I guarded that position jealously.

The accountant had already been nicknamed 'the money man' by some quick minds. The narration of my encounter with him added to the fun of teasing him in his absence. That evening, when he sought out our table, we looked at each other in expectation of more fun. Someone had said, "Here comes the money man," and we readied ourselves for him. We thought he had noticed our table because we made the most noise and laughed the loudest. A man alone at a table of six women, we lavished him with our joy. Laughter came easily as we joked about the day's array of embarrassing displays of ignorance about a subject some of us had taught for years. He laughed with us, was fascinated by the way we were able to laugh at ourselves. He did not seem to be paying particular attention to any of us, which suited us well as a group. After the meal, he offered us drinks at the bar. We happily accepted, since that meant more fun and a saving on our allowance.

The following day, he sent me a note in the seminar room inviting me for dinner outside the hotel. I was surprised, flattered and curious. Somewhere inside, distantly, laughter emerged as I felt the daemon lift its head. Later, when he called my room to confirm the appointment, I said to him, more out of embarrassment for accepting his date so easily than any desire to refuse, "We really do not know each other."

"I know your name. You are Doreen Seko. You teach geography at Sokoni Juu Primary School in Moshi Rural District. Am I correct?"

Of course he had picked the information from my seminar registration form, but to make him feel good, I said, "Yes."

"Mine is Patrick. Martin Patrick," he said.

I agreed to go to dinner with him.

Now, fate having stretched its hand to grip my life firmly, and with the benefit of hindsight, I have come to realize that from that evening onwards, the daemon blossomed and reigned in its kingdom.

Believe in magic, it whispered softly to my mind that night. Believe in magic whose core is life and whose power is beyond rational thinking. Magic which affects life. Life lived, experienced, not by plans and strategies. Believe in magic which births desire and the fear which curbs that desire. Magic that understands survival and Self-preservation, creating the one place in the mind that has sympathy for the softness of the heart....

Martin started courting me, on that first outing at Mount Meru Hotel. I could not have known then, that on that night, I branched onto a road I would walk for the rest of my life.

He talked fluidly about himself, about his two families; that of his mother, separated from his father, and living with his sister and grandchildren; and his father's new family with a young wife, younger than his daughters. He talked of his father's boy children, as young as his grandchildren, smiling pensively, absorbed by a reality he had matured in, one he had accepted. He was once a teacher in the classroom, teaching mathematics, he said, before he studied accounts in order to run away from chalk dust. He talked about friendships and love, about men and women. "I spent my youth with my mother and sisters. My father left us when I was fifteen," he said, pausing, then, "Women are resilient in ways that are quite different from the men," he confessed, shaking his head up and down as if to affirm his own belief. "It was pure miracle that I got an education. Pure miracle!" he emphasized for my benefit. I thought of Godbless then, how much he needed a miracle to happen to his life and it never did. "I sympathize with my father though...," he said, letting the rest hang, as he looked at me. He sounded so worldly - wise. His thoughts flowed smoothly, the words leaving his mouth without effort. He was not much of an eater, perhaps because there was so much passion invested in what he talked about that the food could not compete for attention. I was mesmerized by his ability to talk so frankly about his family matters. Something in him, perhaps the frank nature, the openness, attracted me to him, easing in the sense of familiarity with him that still surrounded me....

Later, we danced.

He did not care much for steps. Put more correctly, he did not know how to dance. He just 'danced' his own style, feeling the music and being led by it. I was relaxed and so I did my thing too until he came close and put his arms around me and then we hardly moved. I think we entered the swift current of the music and were taken by it, losing the sense of where we were, forgetting about people looking at us, flowing smoothly from one song to another. Martin changed after holding my body in dance. I had to leave the floor, pulling myself away from his grip because we had lost the purpose of being on the dance floor. He followed me to our long abandoned seats as though in a trance. Something must have struck him and took possession of his body so that he could hardly sit still. At the lounge couch, he kept saying, *oh, oh, oh,* his glass of brandy sitting untouched. He shook his head and covered his eyes and hummed a throaty tune that was hardly musical. I thought he was drunk.

When he removed his hands from his face and opened his eyes, he said, "Yes, yes, you are here. You are real. Come and sit close to me," but there was no space on the couch for two people to sit, so I remained put where I was. He looked almost sad. "Share my drink," he invited me, with such pleading eyes, I had to comply.

The brandy burned my throat. We talked little.

Later, as we walked back to the hotel in the early hours of the morning, the mystery still in possession of his being, he lifted me off my feet on an impulse, and carried me, walking in the middle of the street, laughing and saying "I feel good. Oh, God, I feel good!"

The reckless voice inside of me whispered, urged, as I laughed hysterically in his arms, throwing both my limbs about like a pampered, spoilt child:

To believe in magic is to release the power of self to realize what is un thought of. And wild. What is desired. It is to release the power in the self to dream. To know the feather lightness of those dreams. To know, and to feel the follies and the heaviness of those follies...

He wanted me to go to his room. I did not dare. He wanted to come to mine. I was more scared, almost screaming out the *no* when he tried to force his way.

"Why?" he asked, quietly, resignedly.

I shrugged my shoulders rather lamely. I did not know the reason, not one that I could tell him. Perhaps I wanted to be sure it was the right thing to do, or I was just afraid of exposing myself to a stranger. I was assailed by doubts, as recriminations from my seminar colleagues rang in my mind and I started imagining the shame I would feel.

'Believe in him!' the daemon pushed. I thought Martin would see me start, as if threatened, as the voice urged. But a stronger instinct held my will and I stood resolutely at the door, fearing to open it lest he force his way in, feeling the conflicting emotions within me. I wanted to dare. I wanted him to hug and caress me. There was, already growing in me, a soft feeling, a feeling with a root and a tenderest shoot, one of fellowship with him, but I was held back by a strong logic which repelled foolhardiness. Finally he said, "Goodnight Doreen."

He turned and went away.

I stood there, rooted to the spot, not saying a word, looking at his disappearing back, regretting, and fighting the urge to call him back. I wondered at a mind that plays a tug of war with itself!

He left the third day after we met. I thought he would give me up, write me off as backward and timid. But he looked for me the morning he left until he found me, made me escort him to the door, holding my hand, made stiff by shyness and worries about social acceptability. He left me all his contacts, the telephones, the department at the ministry where I could reach him, the office extension number, the residence telephone number. He hugged me at the entrance of the hotel, a long, intimate hug. Every one was looking, including fellow teachers at the seminar. I felt nervous, shy and sweaty under the armpits. He whispered, still hugging me, "I will come Doreen. I will look for you at the school. Soon."

The days that followed were filled with energy that made me feel weightless as a feather. I think I was happy, but I did not let the intensity of Martin's feelings seep deep into my skin. I must have instinctively felt the nearness of danger, and was afraid. I kept myself busy. The demands of the seminar and the company of other teachers filled the time. I focused on learning, I wanted to be a better geography teacher. I did not use the telephone numbers Martin left me. I felt a certain absence, yes, a kind of emptiness, but one without the weight of longing. Neither did he call the hotel.

Back at school, I tried to apply my new knowledge in the classroom. I made my teaching aids and insisted that other teachers do the same. I presented a long report to the Headmaster, copying out all the objectives of the seminar as they were given, adding emphasis here and there according to the issue I wanted to push forward.

The Head master was impressed with my report and so he was on my side. It wasn't easy to convince the other teachers. "*He!* Doreen, lower that temperature. You are not the first one to attend a seminar!" one teacher said during lunchtime in the staff room. The others joined in immediately.

"I learned some things that I would like to share," I said, calmly, before I realized that I was facing a hard struggle.

"We shall read your famous report," one male teacher said with a derision that almost made me want to spit in his face!

"Yes, please do. I am sure it will be the first report you *ever* read," I said, my voice blocked by hurt and disappointment. The tension sprang into the air like released spring wire, bringing the female teachers, who were the majority, immediately on my side.

"Ali, who did you quarrel with in the morning? We understand you have no wife and no girl wants you," Anna said. Everybody laughed at Ali's expense, who shot back maliciously.

"You do not want people to know how much you want it from me, do you, and that you can *not* keep away from *my* bed?"

"Hey, hey, hey," Zima interjected quickly, "We are talking about teaching aids here, not things between anyone's legs." The discussion ended in mumblings and grunts.

I realized that the women teachers would be my better allies.

At first, every one of the women had a reason for not making teaching aids. They complained about ordinary things I could even have agreed with before the seminar, especially about not having the time to do it. They were not too enthusiastic because, as they rightly said, everybody treated teachers like mules who have to push themselves forward and survive by the grace of God, carrying the teaching load until they grind to a halt. They thought I was being naïve, and that it was because I was too young in the job. I did not give up on them. "Well, make the best of being mules," I told them. This did not particularly amuse them, but some of them at least managed to laugh in my face, calling me the most stupid girl they have ever met.

A smile comes to my lips just to think of that incident. I would not have the courage to be a good mule today, so I think they were right. Being young made me supple. These days I let things lie if the other teachers have no interest. The Doreen of those days has changed, has at least come to terms with the fact that the rules of life are not always dictated by one's wishes. So I have become a stubborn mule, moving because I hate to be pushed, doing things to protect myself from the lethargy of conformity.

After the failed discussion in the staff room, I invited the women to join a club that was to meet in my place. When they came, I gave each of them some produce from my garden. It was not much, but something offered in goodwill always softens the heart. When I showed them the materials I had collected for making aids, they were beside themselves with laughter. Strings, empty milk tins, egg trays, empty packets of cigarettes, a pile of tree bark, lime, river pebbles... "River pebbles! Where in the world did you get them from?" they exclaimed. The small group agreed that I had gone crazy, but they softened and joined the club. We made a globe from thin tree bark, sewn with thread and bonded together with wood glue. The sand pebbles made maps of Tanzania and its regions on pieces of cardboard and on the cloth- like coconut bark, appropriate for hanging on the wall. We brushed some lime on a big pebble to create the snow capped Mount Kilimanjaro. It looked impressive. The history teacher made excellent baskets out of dry grass while the language teacher discovered she could draw! Her pictures made us laugh but she was very proud of them, and the story she made out of the pictures was gripping. The exercise actually proved enjoyable, it felt like a socializing event laced with gossip in between. It became a very creative exercise that revealed unknown skills. The silt on the bed of our minds, long settled and untouched, was finally stirred. Beautiful things were made, some ending up as decorations for our homes and even for classrooms, to the dismay of pupils. We met every Sunday afternoon and we called ourselves: *The River Pebbles Club.*

That club was really the springboard for my life of struggle, the push to bring change in things and situations, the knowledge that one should not give up before every chance is tried. I never thought that was possible before then. I started believing in myself, in my own capacities. So the next target was the use of books, and with Zima's enrolled support, I appealed to the Headmaster to let the children use library books in the classroom. He looked at me in exasperation, "Doreen, what is it? You want to take over the school?"

"Oh, no, no. Please," I begged, sitting down without being invited, smiling sweetly and appealing for his sense of logic. He smiled back, shaking his head. "You will pay for every book torn or lost," he said.

"I promise to pay for every book torn or lost," I repeated after him, as though I was making an oath of allegiance. I left his office in a hurry and went straight to the supplies teacher. I did not see it then, but I think the products of The River Pebbles Club had won the Headmaster's heart to the new spirit emerging among the women teachers. He personally encouraged the other teachers to use the available books rather than keep them in boxes in the store.

The pupils loved the new liberality. Looking at a new book, opening its pages, clean and not worn out, was for them an experience of happiness. Even when it was a book they knew, they felt as if they had received a present. It did not matter to them that the books were returned to the staff room after classes. I had made a pact with them to use the books carefully so that they were not torn, and so that I could continue bringing the books to class. They watched over each other. Every time I entered that classroom with books in my hands, I could see their eyes enliven with expectation. When I said 'good morning class', their response was charged with enthusiasm. Freshness adds spice to life, I thought, it wakes the mind to greater awareness, higher ambitions, sweeping out the shadows under which staleness thrives. The freshness of the same books they knew lifted the spirit of the class to another plane of expectation and want. I was inspired.

The male teachers who could not deal with the revolution the women had started, asked me, "What happened to you at the seminar?"

They must have seen it in the eyes.

A month later, Martin's letter came.

CHAPTER 4

Words do not grow old like persons do. The test of time does not enfeeble the spirit embedded in them. They live on, perhaps to be dismissed for their irrelevance, or elevated for the truth they continue to render, the spirit of the words changing only in the meanings wrought anew at every reading, perpetually. Looking back and reading Martin's letter, I understand, as though for the first time, what passion is and what it does to us, the marks it leaves behind, the variegated etchings of the face of love.. .

"... I am not going to tell you that I know what love is, Doreen, but I know for sure, that I will forever seek for your love until you offer it to me..." Martin had written. Indeed, wishing and longing is the tinder for magic. More than ten years have elapsed, but the feelings for this man evoked by those words still live in me. Its a more mature longing, one without fire but still alive.

When I received the letter, I must have read it ten times or more. Five long pages of laughing with me, joking with me, dancing with me, five pages of his growing love for me. Martin was a good writer, he knew the right words to use, the right expressions. The impact of the letter on my poor heart was so strong, my mind immediately started to resist. It cannot be true, he cannot love me so, I told myself. He is playing, trying to have fun, he enjoys teasing women, the mind resolved. I put the letter away and busied myself with other things, pushing memories away with self-rebukes, pretending that the experience was a onetime fling. But the self- admonitions did not hold. The daemon inside of me was laughing, conjuring up dreams that woke me up with a start. My will was weak, the logic of the mind was convincing, my heart was aching. The daemon laughed.

His image started sneaking into my mind, forcefully, without effort. I would be standing in front of class, teaching, right in the middle of a sentence, and *pop*, his image would stand before my eyes! And the sentence would evaporate. I thought I was crazy or going crazy. Surely Martin was a person I hardly knew! What was two days of dancing, the feeling of his hand full of tension around my waist and the pressure of his lips on mine? What was this transient passion compared to the steady love and commitment I got from Zima? What was the big thing about Martin carrying me like a child in the middle of the street, shouting to an unhearing world that he loved me? Would that compare with Zima's steady helping hand anytime, for anything? I was being fickle. Zima loved me. He had persevered with me, had been patient and understanding. He would do anything for me, was willing to spend the rest of his life loving me, if only I could agree to marry him. How could I ignore his feelings and feel this way about a man I hardly knew?

The memory of this trying time is a comfort to me now. I believe my heart was right, is still and will continue to be with Martin, because he is the chosen one, the man the living daemon inside me decided to crown with pearls prized from the very matter from which my life is molded. Zima was a practical man who wanted me to give him children and a home he already planned. What would have happened with him and me now that it has come to light that I couldn't give him those children?

That is why I am grateful to my fate, Martin will live with me, and now Joseph has come to my life. He has no pre- prepared plans with me, no great demands, just a subdued, but consistent want of a tired hunter. And there is Milika, the undying bond and symbol of love between Martin and I.

I understand my mother so much now. She decided to fashion her own course in life because she was punished for loving a man, refusing to fit in a mould that would cramp her life. She refused to take loss of love as her lot, refused to believe that loving was wrong and should be punished, even when the man was tamed and failed to stand up for her.

Memory brings me the events of that time, already colored with the stains that time leaves on its path. I remember Zima's reaction when Martin's letter came. He knew immediately that something had created a rift between us. I refused to admit it. There was nothing, I said, there was no one else. We were still very good friends. "Friends!" he scoffed, wanting me to say we are lovers waiting to be married.

Zima had not really been my lover, so there was nothing to deny, but I proceeded to vehemently deny duplicity. What could I have been expecting? The trouble in the lie was the emotion that wrapped my heart as with a soft, warm blanket. It was the unquestioned presence that sat in my mind like a stubborn visitor, waiting, demanding to be served. I questioned my sense of morality, sorcering shame from my actions, from my lack of appreciation of the friendship that was more practical, more tangible and there with me, rather than something that was not yet a relationship.

We argued, Zima and me. We argued about everything, particularly on acceptance and choice in friendships.

"There is no question of choice in friendships, there is only acceptance," Zima said.

The daemon stirred in me, like a soldier called out on duty. "One chooses, one selects friends," I said. "One moves towards certain people, consciously or unconsciously, seeking spiritual contact with the person. We seek for a certain satisfaction, we want to fulfill a certain need in us. The need for friendship is first of all personal, it is based on the desire to satisfy a personal need," I said.

"Friendship has no selfishness. It is the ability to put the other's happiness before yours," he retorted.

"But not as a rule. I cannot do things that will make you happy but make me sad. Not all the time. Neither can you continue accepting your own happiness at my expense. There has to be an extension of Self so that what you do not want done to yourself, you do not do to your friend."

"One can have sex with someone one does not like, because the person one loves is a mess sexually," Zima said, with passion.

"Can't you see? You need sex, satisfying sex. Your partner is no good, but you love her, you say, so you go somewhere else to get what you want. Aren't you satisfying your needs at the expense of what she may feel if she finds out? Do you not see selfishness on your part there?"

"It would be selfishness if I went ahead and loved someone else because of sex and forget her just because we did not hit it off together," he said, completely convinced of his position.

"How can anyone have sex with someone they do not like or love? It is called rape, not sex. There can be no friendship there," I said, desperately.

"Oh yes. There can be friendship without demands, without expectations. One without worries of compromises," he said with such feeling of certainty, all it needed was to show me proof.

"Genuine friendships are expensive, Zima. They entail emotional investments, so expectations have to be there. Even a man who has sex with a prostitute knows he has to pay. There is no friendship there, I admit, but there is expectation. Friendships must be maintained because two people are essentially different in expressions of desires, needs and wants. Each must have room for self expression and therefore both constantly strive not to step into the other's space."

"We are just different in our perceptions of relationships. Period," he said with finality.

"I guess so," I agreed and knew that this discussion would be a landmark in our separate lives. For a long time after this, I carried an emptiness in the pit of my stomach which nothing, not all the endearments Zima had in himself could fill.

I carried Martin's letter in my journeys like a talisman. It was my first serious love letter, not counting the ones illustrated with bleeding hearts that I received in secondary school. I have kept it in a secret file together with the ones I receive from Zima and the cryptic notes Joseph leaves for me when he comes and does not find me at school.

CHAPTER 5

The activities of The River Pebbles Club veered from making teaching aids as gossip took center stage. The neighborhood and the school were fertile grounds for small talk and the women collected these pieces of information like precious beads to bring to the club. This gossip was reported faithfully, enthusiastically, the way patients tell their intimate details of sickness to a family doctor. Laughter was so abundant it covered the nakedness of these details. It was cathartic.

Other sessions were like self - examinations, some kind of group therapy. We started knowing so much about each other, what made us happy, what kind of partners we wanted, our secret loves, hidden weaknesses and fears which were aired in the group with the same reserve that some women have in hanging their underwear out in the sun. The strengths were sung out, proudly, always in comparison to the men folk whose weaknesses were indulgences we laughed at. The men were talked about as if they were naughty young boys needing spanking from their mothers. The club, the sessions, were like a ritual which defined us as a group, an entity with one name. We started rallying together around issues in school to the great surprise of the male counterparts. Our treatment of pupils improved because we were more relaxed and were able to discuss the things that made us punish them.

I did not bring up Martin's name or his coming to these ritual sessions. I did not trust myself, my capacity to talk about a new love I had not lifted from the realm of the heart to bring it to the sobriety of the mind for scrutiny. I doubted the maturity of the group to understand that. I sensed it would be another gossip bead collected for Zima's use. But they soon knew that something was cooking, that I was hiding something from them. I held on, behaving as though I knew nothing, hoping that their curiosity would pass. I did not know how I would respond to the stream of questions from an excited group of women!

"Who is he?" they would ask.

"He is an accountant."

" Uuh, you have made it, Doreen. That one will have money!"

"Who are his people?"

"I don't know."

" Where does he come from?"

" I don't know yet."

"What wealth does he have, you know, a house, a car, a business which he manages after work?"

" I don't know."

No, such ignorance would not do and they wouldn't even believe me. They would laugh, make a joke out of it, use it as a demonstration story to explain the doltishness of village girls. So I saved my face by letting the issue of Martin lie until the whole thing came out on its own.

Not talking about Martin filled the days with expectant daydreaming. Martin lived in my mind. I saw him when I looked at myself in the mirror, felt myself ripen as a strong sex urge washed over my senses like a heat wave. My breasts swelled and their nipples stood on end. And because I felt him in my self like a physical presence, the eyes that looked at Doreen in the mirror were his, the hands that touched the erect nipples, delicately, as if they would crumble, were his. Those hands followed the curve of my stomach, traveled to the elaborate mounds of my buttocks, turning again towards the V where the hairs spread protectively like mulch over seeds just planted. And when the mulch was parted, the ground was wet with expectation....

Throughout the day I imagined how he would look, what he would be wearing, what he would say to me, how he would hold me and kiss me and... I felt again the brush of his warm breath on my neck as he danced with me that night and the memory of his body against mine tightened a hard knot in my guts. And the longing for him grew, mushroomed to a fecund maturity. It occupied space in me, warm and very, very soft. I walked around with it like a young pregnancy. When it became unbearable, the urge to reach this feeling somewhere in the flesh where it sat like an itch was a killing thirst. I longed only to caress it softly, very softly, so that the insistent anguish could subside.

But how did this love break loose from my heart and become public knowledge? What is it that told people I was in love? At school, in the staff room, the male teachers weren't concerned about such a familiar face as mine, they wanted to know about the mysterious man in my life. I must have been a walking mirror that reflected everything I felt inside, the light of its fire must have shone through my skin! How else could they ask such telling questions? I hoped that the agony did not show. The struggle to contain the power of that longing was strictly kept between me and the daemon that had found a dwelling place within the fibers of my flesh and bone, fanning the passion with its own madness.

Zima suffered. The spirit of Martin became a solid wall between his feelings and my person, it shut him out from my mind and thoughts, creating a ring of fire that he could not enter. I was no longer accessible to take his indulgences. He felt abandoned and desolate, like a woman who cooked food for guests who did not turn up.

"Are you in love with *that* man?" Zima asked.

He did not know his name or his person. He had created him, giving him the shape and character of all antagonists. And the created image was real to him, just like the love I felt was a real threat. Was I pregnant? He offered to discuss it, he would be quite open minded with it because sexual weakness is a common human vice, and to save me from embarrassment, he would marry me as soon as possible. The baby would be his.

"No," I said. "I am not pregnant."

"What is it then?"

What could I tell him? That I was in love with a stranger? Martin could be a common city thug, he could be a player looking for excitement and fun. My consciousness pleaded for reason, it told me to quit this nonsense about love and be practical. Take Zima, marry him and run away from this daemon without a form. You will regret it, you will cry for him when he is gone. The insistence in my mind was maddening. Yet, no matter how hard I tried, I could not stop feeling warm and fecund and soft about the stranger called Martin. And the daemon, as if conspiring against the mind by strengthening that unconscious resolve breathed into the heart:

Believe in the power of your own love, which has the potency to surmount doubt and impatience, so you can make real what you desire. Believe in the essence of your feelings, in their meaning, now in the realm of Spirit. Believe in the reason for their being and the necessity for their realization.

One day, I put a stop to the intrigue. "I love a man called Martin," I told Zima.

"What? Who? What are you telling me?"

Up to this day, I cannot describe the emotion I saw on his face. I immediately regretted having made that confession. My mind has told and retold itself the story of Zima and me. The road to love that he walked was too winding, too confusing. He walked it in the mist of cold July, right in the heart of the fog that blurred his sight. My confession surprised him, a cold drizzle on a naked heart in need of warmth. And the heart, so fragile!

What does one do with such tenderness in this hard world?

"I have never felt this way about any man before," I told him.

"So you do not care about me at all? You do not even have shame to tell me in my face that you are in love with another man? I have waited three years for you! Why didn't you tell me that you were not interested?"

Silence was kinder.

"Doreen, you are behaving like a common prostitute! You are sickeningly fickle! Honestly, what has happened to your good sense?"

He was angry. He was bruised. His pain was too tender to be touched and impossible to be healed by the power of any word. We parted in a worse state than before. He started sulking, became rude to me. Finally, he accused me of skipping lessons to the

Headmaster. I was given a stern warning. My face must have worn a mask screening off any feeling because the Headmaster asked, "Are you not going to defend yourself? Don't you care whether you are being fairly treated or not?"

"Every teacher knows that I have not skipped any classes sir. I thought you knew that too," I said.

"Is that all?" the Headmaster asked. "Are you saying that Mr. Zima is not telling the truth?"

I had already decided that I wouldn't have his pain dissected for analysis. So he stood by his story and I stood by mine, aided by silence and sullenness between us that rose and swelled like over leavened bread. He relied on the moral support of a fellow man to understand his case. He was sure the Headmaster would believe his story, and so whatever punishment meted out to me would please him. But some pains are like open ulcers, they cannot be hidden. They bleed openly in uncontained sourness. The Headmaster must have seen this when he looked at Zima and then at me and said, "Doreen, you go. I will call you later."

I did not follow up on what transpired between the headmaster and Zima, but I knew that the truth or a version of it must have been revealed. The next day, the head master told me, "Doreen, this was your first mistake so I will not write you a warning letter. You are a very good teacher and I do not want to hear about you skipping classes again."

I did not respond to that and he did not push me further.

Then gossip bloomed and spread like dust carried by the wind. It caught and thrived, homing in people's imagination. It did not matter who started it all. It did not matter where the stories came from, who spun the versions out like yarn! Everyday!

Why wasn't anyone asking what really happened between Zima and I? Why didn't anyone care for the truth?

I felt their eyes following me, accompanied by giggles that sounded like a shuffling of dry leaves in the wind. I felt like screaming in frustration. If I had had enough courage in me to face what they had to say, I would have asked them if they wanted to know what I felt. Could it be that someone would understand, and be willing to speak out for me, to tell the world that, yes, emotions as intangible as clouds could be gathered and marshaled into a pillow of dreams?

Perhaps my brother Godbless had a point when he said that love is just imagination. "Sex is more real, sister, more tangible, more satisfying. I can never understand love." So, in short, love is something we create in our minds to colour our fancy! The issue then is; why does this flimsy fancy of the imagination drive people wild? Why does it bring out from people the mob urge to persecute those who love? Why is love such a *threat*?

Every kind of spice was added to make the gossip sound more interesting. The story about Doreen's love for a stranger grew in proportions larger than life. I found myself on an island, alone, without a friend to rally around me, in a place where just a short while back I had been the center of attention.

The River Pebbles Club that had been like a drinking place for thirsty travelers in the desert was corrupted by the gossip. Is it true? Really? How come she didn't tell us? Ah, look how she took us for a ride as we told her our own stories! To think she *pretended* to be our friend! To imagine that! Ah, such *hypocrisy*.

The members dropped out one by one and the few who held on to it for what the spirit of the club had done for them failed to cut through the possibilities of untold stories that sat in the room like a separate entity. The trust went with the laughter that had risen from the bosoms of women like spring water rises from the earth. Laughter had come, naturally, because the women had discovered treasures hidden in them. They had not known that they were capable of creating beautiful things out of nothing, that is, out of their own will and the urge to try. The compulsion to fashion new things dried up, the mood was run out of the group like a bad spirit.

When they were all gone, I sat in the room they had sat in and felt lost in it. Two, three, four glasses of cold water could not dislodge the stone that settled in my throat the whole night. The following Sunday I went to church but found no peace. There was only one ally that pushed me to accept the loss and go on with life: my heart was full of love.

The period before Martin's arrival was forlorn, lonely. I appreciated then the work of being a teacher, of struggling together with the children, the teacher trying to impart knowledge, the pupil trying to learn. I was more sympathetic to their inabilities, more patient with their tricks, more understanding of their pains. Loss and alienation made me a better teacher!

So, I lived the life of a lone soul wanting to give to others. After the secret became public, I was seized by the urge to talk. I wanted to share what was bubbling in me, but I had no friend to listen to me. I had more or less lost Zima by loving another man, and the group by withholding the news of that love. I became the underground stream seeking an outlet, struggling to push towards open air, towards the crack in the earth through which it must channel its own current, spring out and flow upon the earth, to be drunk, to cool, to elate... I floated with the daemon inside me, I burned with it, and in that time, I understood its restlessness.

My mother was of course right. "You will know when it comes," she had said, when I had asked her, a long time ago it seems, how it feels to be in love.

I was in secondary school then. My mother always encouraged me to ask her questions about girl things or woman things, things that I thought I needed to understand. I was sure somehow that love was one of the girl things that I could ask my mother about. She had laughed.

We were sitting at the hearth, the pot cooking on the hearthstones. Fire warmed the whole place. There was peace around us at that time when we had finally settled down. Everything would have been done and the boys would be in the other house playing and quarreling with each other at every chance, waiting for food. Outside, it would be pitch dark, the plants in the grove making scary shadows that moved. Now and then there would be the shrill crying of the night bird, or the loud moo-ing of the neighbor's cow, whose call, mother always responded to by saying, 'why don't they feed that cow?!'.

Cows were her friends. The animals contributed substantially to the well being of her life and that of her children. She talked to them like she talked to us, only she was less angry at the cows. She touched their stomachs to know whether they have had enough grass, scolded them when she thought they were being gluttonous. She praised them when they gave enough milk, and worried terribly if their udders got sick. Cows were very present in our lives. Other than that presence in the darkness, the night was like a warm wall around the out kitchen where the fire and the murmurings of the cooking food softened our mood as we talked quietly to each other.

That day, mother did not respond to my question. She went on with her business of touching this and that, feeding the fire with firewood, quarreling with the cat that constantly meowed around her legs like a jealous lover demanding total attention.

As my mother's only daughter, we had become friends over time. I had learned to confide in her and she had learned to tell me things that I knew she did not tell other people. That was not often though. Only sometimes she would be in a certain mood that made her talk, then she talked to me about the life of a woman.

She talked about how important it is for girls to aspire to learn and know new things of the world. "If I had enough education, you think I would be here?" she said. I tried to imagine where else she would be, what she would be doing. She warned me about putting all my expectations and trust on just any relations. "They will throw away your dreams like they throw cow dung in the grove," she said, sounding angry. "Girls should learn to work hard, always. Hard work will be their salvation." She told me that the world has very little to give girls for free, that they should never, *never* let people walk on their heads and kill their spirit before they know who they are.

Mother spoke generally about girls, as if I was different from the rest of them, as if I was just a girl to whom she was offering advice. She was never specific about herself either. She would talk about the *life of a woman* as if what she said affected her only generally, not specifically. Nothing she told me was specific to me! I understood her clearly much later, after I was married. I came to know that my life as a woman would be realized ultimately, and in so many ways, in relation to other women. She meant that my life would always be a landmark for a girl growing up, or for others needing a role model. She was telling me that my life must strive to give meaning to others needing it. When my life dissolved into Martin's family life, so easily, like sugar dissolves in water, I realized with a pang, that my mother was saying that I will always live out my struggles in relation to other women, women's lives and their perceptions of it, their society and their niche in it, their relations with men.

My mother spoke so little, her wisdom packed into such few words, it took me years to comprehend. She knew that I would meet friends, colleagues at work, in - laws and others in marriage. She knew too that I would either be influenced by them and their thoughts or I would stand up for what I believed in, if I had it in me. Her rendering of emotional experiences were often wrapped in gestures, making as if she were throwing the bitterness of her life experience away in the corner of the out kitchen where she collected the dirt she swept in the night for removal in the morning.

When my curiosity to understand in depth something she said was raised to an aching point, I went to Great Aunt Mai. She was the oasis that Godbless and I went to for most of our emotional needs.

Only once, however, did Mother talk to me about a man, his behavior and manners, how he worked hard and what he owned, what he gave to others. I did not relate the "others" to her, and at the point of telling, it did not matter. She made it feel so beautiful and distant, it was as if she was talking of a man from a folk tale or a legend. I gave him a face and character that I liked and that corresponded with mother's story. My creation did not at all look like one of the men of the village that I met on the road, walking bare foot, with dry skin and uncombed hair, smelling of smoke from cigarettes rolled from pieces of old newspapers. It didn't. He was handsome, soft spoken and charismatic. He smelled of freshly washed and ironed clothes and he smiled to my mother. That was the color and imprint I gave to her story, and my child's instincts were pulled to it unreservedly, without analysis. She smiled when she talked of this man and her eyes stared in the fire. The softness of her mood and voice when she talked of him could have awoken me to see a woman in love. But then I was a child, and I did not understand the human situation and the ways of the spirit beyond what the ears received. Later, upon reflection, I realized that I had not comprehended in any concrete way much of what mother said. Human life was like an onion, and I had not known that one does not know the onion without the knowledge of its layers.

Now, my mind turns those stories up, like soft earth yielding to cultivation and seeding. The plots of my mother's stories, arch into mine so that I recreate them from the raw matter of my own life. It really feels like turning up the earth again in a new season, earth ready for planting, the stored warmth in it meeting my hands and feet in convivial greeting between good friends. As a young girl, that world, my mother's, was far removed from the angle of my naïve lenses of life. Now, they converge, only the angle changing slightly to distinguish my situation from hers. She must have known then, as she talked softly looking into the fire, that she could not package the definition of love in a formula that she could hand over to me and say, there, Doreen, my daughter, that is how it feels to be in love.

My mother had four children by men who did not marry her. I had not seen any man come home and yet my mother got a child. I resolved to find out how this happened so when I went to collect bananas from Aunt Mai's home for my mother's food after the third child, Alfred, was born, I asked Great Aunt Mai, "How come our father does not live with us?"

Aunt Mai said, "What do you want me to tell you?"

"Where does he live? Don't fathers live at home with their children?"

She put the basket of bananas dripping with sticky, thick sap on my head and said, "Go and cook for your mother so she can get her strength back. Go good girl."

"But where does our father live, Aunt Mai?" I insisted and refused to make another step until I received an answer.

"*Ya*! What kind of child are you? Why do you want to know all this?"

She was uncomfortable, I could see. I wondered why this was a secret that should be hidden, like the human nakedness we were always urged to hide. Nakedness was supposed to be ugly, but when I looked at myself or at Godbless when he bathed on Sunday, nakedness was not ugly. So why should a part of our lives be such taboo?

"Now, a woman who has just given birth should not be hungry. The milk will dry up, so run and take the bananas home so she can have food, then come back again and I shall tell you," Aunt Mai promised.

I went home thinking about this secret. Why us? All my friends' fathers lived at home with their mothers and the children. What was the problem with us?

When I went again, on a Sunday, so Aunt Mai would have no excuse for not telling me, she swore me to secrecy and told me about the men my mother had children with. Aunt Mai did not condemn my mother. She said it in a matter of fact way that my brother Godbless and I shared a father. The one who was just born had a different father. How did she know all this, I wondered. How come we who lived with our mother did not know? Later still, when the last one, Samson, was born, I never associated mother with any man who looked like the child. We knew, at a certain time, that she was pregnant, but not when or how. When she was almost due to have the baby, she would prepare a few things, baby clothes left over from the last one, and, one day she would tell us she was going to hospital. I was the one instructed to inform the neighbor and Aunt Mai that she was due. Indeed, in late afternoon or the early evening the neighbor and mother would come back with the baby. Both times, the neighbor woman and I took care of mother until she was strong again.

My mother would be excommunicated from church every time she became pregnant. Aunt Mai said it was because mother had committed a sin. "What sin, Aunt Mai?" I had asked.

"You would not know it even if I explain. Only adults understand the sin," Aunt Mai had told me.

"What will happen to her then?" I asked in concern, wondering why mother continued to commit the adult sin. "Will the church punish her?"

"Before the baby is baptized, your mother will go to the pastor and confess. The pastor will ask her if she has held council with herself to realize that she sinned against God and will not sin again. Your mother will say, yes, she has held council with herself and that she will never sin again. The pastor will pray for her and she will receive forgiveness from God," Aunt Mai explained. Mother would then be re-returned to church to baptize the child. I never understood the logic of doing this, it sounded like an adult game played after committing an adult sin. It didn't sound too serious either, and after all, all of us had good Christian names. We went to Sunday school and were all registered for confirmation so that we would be taken into the church as individual adult members.

The thirst to know what love was all about had not been quelled. When I went to secondary school, I started unraveling, on my own, the secrets that had surrounded us about babies and secret ways of having them with men who were invisible. One day, I asked mother again about being in love and she responded rather impatiently, "Do you have a boy?"

"Well, eh may be," I stalled. "But how does it *feel*, mama?"

That is when she told me to wait for the time to come.

Of course I was not happy with that answer. I thought my mother was being unfriendly or that she did not want me to have boy friends. I thought the time had already come for me because I had a boyfriend. All my friends at school had boyfriends. Some of the older girls who had older and worldly wise boyfriends had even been with the boys and had seen them naked! Now, that was something! I burned with curiosity to know how they look, how their *thing* behaves? What happened when a boy and a girl were together in a secret place?

Girls told each other stories at night about things some of us younger ones were not allowed to hear. My boyfriend had told me how he loved me dearly, had sent me letters full of bleeding hearts pierced by arrows and had put red rose petals in the envelope. Of course I had written back with bigger drawings of the hearts and arrows and infused proclamations of deep love.

When we met, mostly when he came to school to see me on a

weekend or when our school went to theirs on a social evening, we were hardly able to sit together for long. I was too shy, he was too nervous. I could not look at his face for more than a minute, could hardly bear his eyes on mine. We never touched, we did not know where to touch and to avoid doing the wrong thing, would sit a good distance from each other.

In boarding school, girls learned how to kiss from the more experienced ones, but I never learned. I found the practical aspect of it quite unbecoming. I could not embrace a girl and pretend she was a boy, and then kiss her and pretend to feel enamored. So I did not know how to kiss a boy and I was afraid to risk experimenting just in case I did it the wrong way and became pregnant. He too was timid or perhaps he was as ignorant as I was. Parting brought tears to my eyes and to him, helplessness. He begged me not to cry, he promised to marry me the moment we finished school. It was so hard for me to think that my heart would ever respond to love for another man. It was hard to imagine that the eyes would ever see beauty in another man. This meant more letters, sometimes a letter a day as a way of venting what we could not do. The letters from both sides were accompanied by presents like colorfully embroidered handkerchiefs, biscuits, chocolates, and sometimes, when he had pleaded enough with his kin, and someone had sent him money, he bought me perfume.

I was so convinced then, that he was the love of my life, to be treasured until I die. No one else was like him! I wanted my mother to give this colorful bubble some solidity, to tell me that the bubble was made of something hard and precious, to give it a name. I meant to continue with letter writing, and I needed to define my feelings in those letters, in the drawings of colorful flowers supposed to show him the degree of my passion for him. I needed to draw from mother's wisdom and knowledge, so I pressured her further, "How did you *feel* when you loved *my* father?"

I chide myself today for being that daring and naive. Would I ever detail to Milika, how I loved her father? Would I have the words? What words would I use to transmit to her that experience of sinking into self? Would I tell her that my experience is an exception or a general rule?

My mother looked me in the eyes, not believing her ears, and said, as severely as she could, "Child, I *am* your mother!"

I was taken aback then by that severity. I was confused by the enormity of my mother's reprimand. What did I ask that was so wrong?

She had said, "Prepare the dishes for dinner," summarily dismissing my feelings and me.

I never asked her again and she never brought it up. And in time, the boy of the bleeding heart was swallowed by the world that takes young people after school. I also disappeared into the same world and we never knew where the other was. The idea of marriage died a natural death because none of us pursued it or even thought of it as other more immediate things occupied our minds. The feeling of the bleeding heart had somehow moved from the heart to another place.

When a man finally came, I didn't stop to look at life, I lived it the way it came. It felt good to see him feel good so I learned to say what pleased him. I thought it was normal to please, it was what was expected and so did not feel remorse for the 'little lies' that came as part of relating. Was it sex that changed things? Or was I more grown up? What was love and what wasn't? What was right?

When Martin stumbled into my life, the only thing I was sure of was what I felt. I forgot everything about bleeding hearts showered by a profusion of red rose petals. I would have failed if I were asked to put my feelings about Martin in words. After living with him, I came to know that the bleeding heart came later, for me and I think for him too. It came when desires for each other started crusting like the skin of a bad ulcer, when our life became predictable, and the demands of the social system that defines who a male person is, those social expectations piled upon the man became the cutting knife of his identity as a *real* man, when the home became a forest in which we were both lost, calling to each other, but failing to reach out and hold hands. No amount of love I felt for him could exempt him from those social expectations. No amount of it could soothe his inability to meet the test.

Good memories are like a warm, comfortable bed after a tiring day. They receive the tired soul, like a mother who takes a child that runs to her for safety into her cuddly embrace. Good memories say: here, everything will be okay again. They open windows and so hope gets an extended lease. I often recall that time Martin came to Sokoni Juu Primary School and the daemon woke in me like something bruised by tethered passion. It breathed, urgently, into my soul:

Exaltation must be received when it is offered, it must be shared, so that the soul can open its doors to beauty...

That was the time I clearly knew that the daemon was a force in me that wanted its way. My mind had no control over it. I started listening to this force, talking to it in a way that made me act mad, only I did it in private.

The morning of Martin's arrival was no different from any other day. I woke up, bathed and anointed my body with oils and lotions before the mirror. I asked the mirror's reflection, 'whose face is that? Whose eyes?' A gentle breeze was blowing, the cool air finding my soft skin through the window. Love in my heart had made my body fecund, attractive. I looked at it in a new way. I wanted to feel it, touch every part of it, because it had attained magic that pulled my eyes to it. And the daemon sang:

> *A woman's body is beautiful,*
> *A woman's body is magic.*
> *A woman is the earth and the sun in union.*
> *She is the moon and the sea in union.*
> *A woman is the depth and the surface of passions.*
> *Her body is the entrance to mystery and myth.*

I was amazed that the body was mine. It was a treasure house full of rooms and surprises. I dressed it in a bright red dress.

That was the day the whole school held its breath as I received and welcomed the total stranger into its midst. He came directly to the school, to my total surprise and shock. It was overwhelming. I could not stop him from embracing me. I was not used to men who loved women openly and hugged them in public!

And why didn't I resist, refuse to be embarrassed by this urban display of affection?

As I entered the circle of his arms, as if by sorcery, I felt the silence of the whole school give way to a wave of noise that frothed at the shore of communal expectation. Faces, innocently naughty like baby monkeys, peeped through the shutter-less windows. Who is he? Where does he come from?

I was a knot of emotions, shy, embarrassed, confused, happy. I moved in one tight knot as I finally steered him into the staff room where I was too tongue-tied to speak, so he had to introduce himself.

From that moment onwards, time moved outside myself. When it was already night and we had eaten, and for the first time since I knew him, had gathered enough courage from somewhere in me to allow and accept him to sleep with me, I steered Martin towards the bedroom. Something else, not my mind, took over and guided the rationality of my actions so that I undressed as he did, touched his naked body with my hands and with my whole body, tasted his kiss and faced the raw truth of our passion as we entered a cloud somewhere in space.

Martin ripped both my life and my body open, feasting on it like a starved child. I lost consciousness of the co-ordinates of the body that had been concretely mine and in my control just that same morning. A switch had activated our bodies into a state of madness. Martin was possessed. His body was electric and wild. Afterwards, when the energy had been spent, flashes of sobriety crossed my mind like moving sunrays, and I asked myself where he came from? Was he real?

I was mesmerized, captured in the grip of such strong passion. I was entranced. I felt like an overripe fruit, juicy, sweet, tender and willing. We lived, night and day, riding airless clouds. I scandalized my colleagues and my neighbors in the sudden, shameless indulgence. *Hm*, who is this man? they asked themselves. Doreen never behaved so immorally, just like a whore! But then I had become blind to stares and side whispers, to insinuations and outright rudeness from housemates, both women and men. A sense of rebellion had come to flower around a pleasant calm, a quiet peace. The daemon was appeased.

Zima went under, like those rivers that suddenly disappear, leaving behind only a dry riverbed covered by a vacuous silence of sand and stones. The vanished river could bed on a rock in a cul de sac, where the earth's incline and a boulder would wall its way and stay its force. Or, the river could move on, as its nature is to never relent, to never stop, finding an accommodating channel within the dark warmth of the earth through which it courses its way until it surfaces again, miles away from its original course.

That was the week Martin and I decided to get married.

PART TWO

Daemon at the Hearth

Intercourse is an activity heavily regulated by law...
Breaking the law is widely construed as anti social,
forbidden acts are said to hurt society as a whole;
they are social, not private. *Intercourse has never been*
comprehended by law as a private act of personal freedom...

Andrea Dworkin
Intercourse, 1987

O ur wedding was a simple affair conducted at the District Commissioner's office and witnessed by two friends of Martin's. The best lady was a distant relative of his. I did not have friends in Dar es Salaam and could not think of a relative who would be willing to undertake the part. That did not matter to me because if someone would have asked me then, I would have said that Martin is my closest relative.

We did not dress formally like normal brides and grooms do. I wore a simple dress, soft cotton, with light pink floral patterns against a white background. My shoes were also white. I looked like a grown girl going to Sunday school. Martin dressed in blue trousers, white shirt and red tie. He looked handsome and very, very vibrant as if charged by a battery. The best lady, Farida, wore an elegant, brightly colored kitenge dress which left her gold adorned neck open to the parting of her breasts. Sosi, Martin's friend was dressed exactly like Martin. We were our own photographers, Farida and Sosi taking turns, and sometimes we asked a person who happened to be around to take a group photograph.

We sat on the bench outside the District Commissioner's office, on the first floor of the building. No one around was concerned about the wedding. It was a normal Saturday in the office. I remember experiencing some moments of sadness because it felt like we were being forced by some circumstance not to hold a 'normal' church wedding. The waiting made me nervous, but Farida kept my mind busy talking about elegance in women. She found fashion shows absolutely important because they display just how beautiful women are and how color was invented just for them. She spoke enthusiastically, poking me with her hand every now and then for attention. She said I looked as good as any model, and if I were not getting married, surely modeling would have been a good area to try my luck.

Farida liked gossip. She was endowed with a powerful imagination and a neat capacity to remember people, especially women she met, even once, what they wore- dress, head gear, shoes, makeup, nail polish - and would reproduce what they said. She talked about their men and lovers, how they matched or mismatched. I did not ask how she got that information because nothing she said was important. She got incredibly spicy news from hair salons that she kept reproducing, enjoying the monologue of her own yarns. In confidential tones, she confided to me how lucky Martin must be to get me because I really was quite naïve and innocent, not like town girls.

Sosi and Martin were less talkative. They stood with their hands in their pockets and only talked occasionally, often in response to questions they put to themselves.

The ceremonial room looked drab and small, bearing no resemblance to a church with an elegant design and a mood of holy ambiance lending mystique to religious rituals. The room shouted its identity. It was a government office, whatever happened in the room fell in the routine of ordinary government activity, without individuality or variation. My mind registered the state of the place and released it immediately. Really, what mattered was the *essence* of this ceremony, not the place it was being performed!

The office had a long table, centrally placed, with six chairs. The government official sat against the window at the head of the long table, a bible on his right hand and a ledger on his left. He looked somber; almost detached from the ceremony, as if stating in clear body language that he bears no responsibility to the consequences of the union he was about to preside. I noted his detachment and a doubt pushed through my mind, aggressively but briefly, whether this was what I really wanted. But again, I comforted myself with the thought that as long as Martin was by my side and ready to marry me, nothing was going to worry me. Not the somber face, the dust in the room, the cobwebs on the walls or the drab piles of files, possibly abandoned records, which occupied a whole wall behind us. The only thing of color in the room was a bouquet of plastic flowers on the table. They did lift the mood of the room somehow, standing mute, at the center of the table like an unfailing sign of hope.

I have participated in and attended weddings after my own, and have come to affirm that wedding ceremonies are just that. Ceremonies. They are often staged for show, to assert social status, owned or desired, for the records, later to add to the marriage cv. This is later reappraised every time the visitors come, inspecting the photographs displayed at strategic places in our sitting rooms and through photo albums offered to them as entertainment. The photographs or the elegance of the wedding day no longer counts in the quality of life the newly weds lead. It could of course be that

I have become wiser or that I have lost the innocence and naiveté Farida observed in me that day.

The serious official welcomed us to the occasion, trying to look cheerful but unhurried. He put on the jacket that had draped the chair he sat on, looking suddenly changed upon adding the black jacket against the yellow tie. As he straightened his tie, Farida adjusted her gold chains on her full, shining bodice. She sat across the table with Sosi, so she could not stretch over to dab my face like all matrons do to brides during the ceremony. But, even that did not matter. It was enough that we were getting married, that we were going to live together every day of our lives. It did not matter either that there was no song, no choir singing its heart out for me.

The official preached quite convincingly. He talked about love in marriage, about devotion and commitment to each other, about respect for the family and the institution of marriage, which is its pillar. The pastor would have said the same words, only in a different tone. Was it the pastor's costume, the sing-song voice, the church scene that simply made church weddings special? The official spoke well, but he did not inspire. I could feel the impatience in both of us as he went on and on. We knew what he was saying already and we wanted him to end the occasion; he could not replace the church.

But twin to that sense of urgency in myself that wanted the official to hurry, was another side, more patient and respectful, that was listening and following the official's words. Fleeting questions, like falling leaves, passed through my mind: Is marriage and family part of the same thing? What relates them? What did I learn about marriage and family from my mother? What difference could it have made if we had all been born of one father within a marriage?

Oh, but Godbless would *have* the father he so desired. This had been the shadow over our lives, that we were fatherless because mother was not married. Perhaps that was the difference? A girl had to get married so that her children could *qualify* to have a father? I felt lucky that my many children would have a father. I felt a surge of warm feeling for Martin, for giving me this chance to give my children a father. In that moment, as if to receive the feeling like a present, he held my right hand with both his hands below the table. I could feel his heart beats like flapping wings upon which his expectations rode in the glory of that moment. I felt his reassurance through the pulse of his heart and the thin sweat of his hands and I loved him so much then. What he was feeling was one with a strong current inside him that came to me in the locked fingers under the table. I felt completely secure with him.

Finally, it was our turn to speak. We made our vows and put the rings on each other's fingers. The four of us signed the book and so, Martin and I became man and wife.

The happiness I felt that day became a presence that lodged at the corner of my heart and stayed, always to remind me, in those moments of doubt, that I love Martin and will always love him. After the ritual, and as we lived as husband and wife, the door of my soul opened to him and he came in and out as he wished. I did not know, and it did not matter, whose thought paths pulled the other, but an instinct told me that long ago, when both our spirits were searching, when the search was yet unconscious, some chip from him came to meet my spirit and found a home. I knew too that the mystery in his quiet personality, the sensitivity and softness of character, the vulnerability when he is uncertain or unhappy, the surprising hardness openly displayed when he is determined to have his way would keep me by him, wanting to know his passions, long into our future.

That is why I lose my bearings in the winding lines of our story. I revisit the mood of that day often, and wonder how having or not having a child came to be engrained in the vows he made. What could have killed magic in the heart of the man who would search for my love for the rest of his life? What came to cloud the passion, the knowledge paths he undoubtedly took me through, moving, as in osmosis towards the place of magic in the female body?

The sun shone bright the day I was married. Birds chirped among the few tree branches at the District Commissioner's office and people laughed as they went about their business. Marriage in a government office was no crowd puller, passersby looked at us curiously, noting the simplicity of the occasion. Martin hugged and kissed me passionately, calling me Mrs Patrick, Mrs Patrick, as if he could not believe it was true. His temples pulsed. It felt like he could burst with the sheer expanse of joy in his heart. I laughed and I cried at the same time, seeing him so happy. In the fever of elated emotions, he lost control of things and Sosi took charge of the occasion. A taxi took us to the Seaside Hotel, laughing at Farida's jokes, which just fit the mood. We sat at a table on the beach under a big umbrella. The waiters were surprised to learn that it was a wedding, with a record crowd of four people. We told them that it was all we had money for. We were so happy; they changed their minds about the relevance of big weddings and later told us that ours was a good idea. The miracle that Jesus performed on the mountain when he fed thousands on five loaves of bread happened to us that day. We had lunch and then drinks and dinner and we danced until four in the morning without getting into debt. We let Sosi and Farida go while we stayed in the same hotel, lost ourselves in ourselves as we made love, made great, indulgent and wonderful love, the whole of the following day.

CHAPTER 7

I like to call the few weeks following our wedding, the weeks of dream. We planned and built our future from strong bricks of wishes and desire. We wanted four children, two girls and two boys, a bigger house than the one Martin already had and a big farm where we could grow things and keep animals so I would not miss home.

Martin was magic. What else should I call someone so fluid, so deeply resonating with feeling? He talked about our life together, the children we would have and how we would raise them. He talked about our parents, how to reconcile the wrongs done to our mothers. His hands touching a part of my body all the time as he talked. We lived, naked for whole days, not knowing whose body was whose because we had lost the sense of individual selves and had become one. We explored the landscapes of our bodies, traveling over the plains and up the mountains and through the forests. We swam in the rivers, frolicking in the deep ends like the blessed fish. We basked on the beaches, encouraged by the softness of their curves and mounds, shining like oiled guards under the sun of laughter and kisses until the skin tinged with tension and heat from touch.

A window to the inner Martin opened, into the person Martin.

I wondered at how much of the richness of feeling and knowledge was in him. How many doubts and fears about the unknown aspects of life he harbored. He was not the accountant he was known to be. Money codes, balance sheets, cash flows and budgets and deadlines had fled from us, fled from the enveloping peace that left no room for anything else. Being at home for whole days, we found time to play and discover ourselves.

He talked. "Men make a big mistake when they invade a woman instead of walking in, slowly, carefully, calling to be welcome. Waiting to be met at the door," he said.

My mind didn't register what we could have been doing or where we were. We could have been in bed or having breakfast or lunch or dinner. "A woman's body is really like the earth, it has soft ground that is tender and pliable; and it has hard rock too. There are courses of clear rivers whose currents rumble with vital life. The source of all this, men would give the world to know and to own."

I looked at him talk and wondered where the poetry was coming from, what was prompting the words from inside his head. He looked completely relaxed, totally at peace with time and place. He would stare at me, and if he were not near enough, would come closer and touch any part of me and be quiet, for a long time.

"I love to see you like this. I love to hear you talk," I would say quietly.

And my body also sang its poem.

Sometimes he talked as he walked around, looking outside through the window or walking to the bathroom, naked but not naked. He turned off the radio and anything that produced sound not coming from our two selves. Friends came, knocked and went away thinking we were out.

"A man has to search for those things, *must search* in order to know a woman. He must leave the ego at the door before he enters," he said.

Both my hands propping up my chin, hands digging on the thighs for support, sitting on the bed, watching him prepare dishes on a side table so that we can eat strange food we had boiled. There was no time to cook sensible food. We ate out when we wanted. Thinking: only love, never lust, can reveal such a road to a man, only love can take him through the maze of instincts so sharp and prone to change. Thinking: I will take him for a swim in the deep; we will frolic in the warmth born of the tenderness of our desires.

And he said, "Often, men go into a woman to ply, to quarry, to scavenge, hitting the hard rock instead, wasting their energy on blind passion full of froth..."

He felt so gentle, so impossibly big and spiritual. My eyes water just to think of the subjugation of that tenderness in Martin. Why did he arrest the search for that magic? Why did desire for a boy child scare him into abandoning home?

Would he admit that he now goes to quarry like he said he did to me in Sokoni Juu?

"Yes," he had said. "The first time, I was full of froth. God, I was a trapped dam that needed release. I am sorry," so quietly said, nestling his head between my breasts. "You are forgiven. You are forgiven," I saying those words, feeling his soft, beautiful core with my whole being.

I have wondered often if that was a confession, brought up by the feeling of being totally enveloped by a woman's love that must have ripened his body and spirit to a maturity of the senses. Wouldn't that kind of thing be only temporal, after which he would have to escape the pain of the sharply focused intuition?

But still, the memory cushions my hurt with warmth, it soothes my parched soul so that the stories that live in my head are released, coming alive to pry the heart, looking for an act of grace in it all to enable me to continue loving.

Yes, I knew God, and I knew heaven, in the time just the two of us lived together until his sister came and worked hard to make Martin a good husband for me and me a good wife, because she loved both of us so. Three weeks after the sister had come and settled, the mother came, full of joy and ululation. Her son had secured a kitchen for himself, she said. A home is the hearth, the place where the woman makes fire and cooks herself into the husband's heart. Don't people say the road to a man's heart is through the stomach? She brought a little girl, a relative, to live with us as house help.

Before I had time to look and see where Martin had gone, I was grazed into my place in the kitchen while the man of the house was run from the home to bars and those other places where real men go to talk about running and managing affairs of substance. I started looking after the home, had to make sure that all the people ate and the house was clean and the guests were made happy. People came to visit, all the time. They called me *Mama Patrick*. Friends and neighbors called him Martin. His mother and sister called him *baba*.

Did I change? Did I see him changing? Did the magic in our life go, threatened into hiding by social norms which defined our place in the web and in which we put more trust than in our hearts?

CHAPTER 8

My mother-in-law had come to take her son and daughter-in-law home so the clan would rejoice and celebrate the important event together. His sister was to remain in Dar es Salaam and look after the house together with the little girl. Martin was not happy somehow, and upon probing him to talk when we were finally alone in the bedroom, he said, "My family situation disturbs me. Where shall we go, to my father's house or to mother's?"

"To your mother's house, of course. She is the one who has taken the trouble to come and take us home, so it goes without saying," I said with all the confidence of logic.

"It is not at all easy," Martin said and kept quiet, as if my reasoning was no good.

He discussed the issue with the mother and sister the following day. I sat near him and left the talking to them since I was too new and ignorant of their situation to comment. The discussion immediately dampened their spirits, falling on the light mood and laughter like cold dew. Then I realized how sensitive the matter was and why Martin avoided talking about it except on rare occasions. I continued to serve them beer, expecting that after the third bottle the subject would be manageably discussed. It was agreed that we would first go to the mother's house the night of the arrival and then Martin would visit his father alone before he took me to his place.

We planned to stay for only a week. On the first day of Martin's leave from work, we took the bus to Songea, from where we would take another bus to Mbinga. It was a long and tiring journey. Once in a while we talked, but Martin was generally quiet, contemplative. His hand on my lap offered him comfort so I held it there, caressing it with mine every now and then. His mother sat away from us. She went to sleep almost immediately after the bus left the station.

Mbinga, in south eastern Tanzania, is hilly and fertile, a coffee growing area full of streams and natural vegetation clothing the hills where people had not cut the trees to start new coffee farms or to build new homes. The elder sister was home but was very surprised to see us. She was unprepared for guests. The children, of various ages and gender were covered with dust, with innocent looking faces and bright eyes, curious at the sight of a stranger coming home with their uncle and grandmother. After the surprise, the sister welcomed us with a short ululation that told the neighborhood of our arrival. She welcomed us into the house and after greetings ran out to get something for us to eat. Mother-in-law stayed with us to talk, mainly to Martin, asking him whether he remembered this or that, an old man or woman who had died in his absence.

I strayed from their conversation, looked around the room and outside in the garden, wondering whether I would get used to the place as home. I looked at the children as they surrounded Martin and their grandmother. I thought: I will be supposed to know their names and their needs and sometimes what to do with their lives.

Their mothers will expect me to be interested in their well-being and even proactively suggest that I take them with me. Martin gave them the presents we had brought, holding them up to know which was going to who. The sister-in-law helped by calling out their names, one by one. She knew all of them, how old, thin, fat, short or tall each was. They were beside themselves with excitement. The mother-in-law beamed with pride. This was *her* son, who had been left to her to raise alone and now was grown and 'rich'. He showed that he cared, even for his nephews and nieces who were other men's children.

The sister-in-law, called Rebeka, had prepared excellent food, *ugali* with dried fish within the shortest possible time. We sat down to eat, together with all the children who ate from one big plate and bowl. They sat on a mat on the earth floor, automatically falling in place, showing that the order and manner of sitting was a daily ritual. I ate from the same plate and bowl as Martin, while the sister and mother ate together. Were it not for the language barrier that prevented me from joining in the laughter, I would have felt one with them. Martin did not help, he left me to cope on my own, but I knew, as he did, that this was not yet the time for him to help me adapt into his family.

After the meal, Martin went to buy beer and soda at the local shop and the feasting and laughter started in earnest. The neighbors came and joined us. Men and women welcomed us over and over, forcing me to greet them and respond to their greetings in their language. They congratulated Martin's mother and sister who beamed with happiness. Mother-in-law, stood up as head of the family and said, "My people, my son here, Martin, has brought us a daughter. Let us receive her with both hands; let us carry her like we carry a baby born into the family so that she can bring blessings into this home." One woman stood and ululated, dancing and singing and in no time almost the whole crowd had joined in. Martin sent for local brew and everybody drank their fill.

In the course of all this, plans changed. Martin did not first visit his father alone the following day. He insisted we go together, escorted by Rebeka. His father's home was on another of his farms nearby. The father's house was no different from the mother's, except that it was newer and smaller. It was a two roomed house built with mud and roofed with corrugated iron. He had already received the news that his son had come with a wife, and somehow, he was expecting us. My heart went out to him, sympathizing with the fact that he could not be there joining in the merry making. Was he not part of the clan?

He welcomed us in after shaking our hands like one does to official guests. He was happy but did not show excitement. Something seemed to disturb him. I could see it as father greeted the son, the disturbance standing between them as each failed to meet the other emotionally. Two young boys, one aged about four years and another about five came running from some place in the neighborhood. They stopped at the door of the house and stared without greeting until the father shouted to them to greet their big brother from the city. It seemed like Martin had not been home for a long time, because the children almost doubted that Martin could really be their brother. It showed in the hesitation and the reserved greeting. Martin tried to charm them by holding and tickling them and enticing them with the possibility of taking them to the city with him in order for them to laugh, be joyful and relax.

In the meantime, I stole glances at the father. He was a tall, thin man who on the face of it looked weak but the energy in his voice and movements said quite the opposite. His hair was completely white, his skin had started to wrinkle and wither except on his face. He did not have much flesh on his body, but particularly on his face, no marked age lines, only an ashen dullness and loss of color and shine told how old he could be. He talked without gesticulating, his hands lying limply on his lap. He took the posture, perhaps habitually, of a man who was always being forced to plead his case. In that, he looked tired but not totally defeated. He was like one who must continue to carry a load home because to leave it on the roadside would be to admit failure and lack of purpose.

His wife had not appeared. He noticed her absence and sprang up calling, "Mama Joni, where are you?"

"I am coming," she said from some place in the inner yard. Finally she came, shy and timid, bent her knees to the floor and greeted Martin, then me and lastly, Rebeka. She did not look directly at our faces. She sat down on the earth floor by her husband's chair and kept completely silent.

Perhaps she was above eighteen, she did not look it. She would definitely pass for the age of the man's grandchild. Pretty, dark, healthy, with long hair plaited in two braids on her head. She had very smooth skin. She did not wear a bra, her bust was full. Once, she looked up and smiled at something Martin had said and I noticed the perfect set of milky white teeth. Martin could not talk to her. I realized why she was not talking. People talked about her life and that of her children to other people and not her. Rebeka presented greetings from her mother to the family, addressing her father, not once looking at the young woman or mentioning her name. Martin talked to his father about how the children had grown, how his wife looked just like when Martin had seen her last. Her husband smiled ruefully and said, without looking at her, "Bring the guests some tea."

She rose and went out. I noticed that she was pregnant.

I have never stopped wondering about where the power and weaknesses of those two women towards their man lay. Whether the power and the weakness were in fact embedded in the man they struggled to claim, and not in themselves at all. The older wife was a strong, determined woman. A woman fired by an anger she could have used to fight her abandonment so that the bitterness would not have come to settle. The younger one, shy and meek, had committed her life to living with a man whose ability to provide for her and her children was fast declining. Both fought for the man through the sons. I wondered which of the women had won or would finally win, and how. What choice did the man have in the life he was living if he had been driven to it only by the desire for sons?

When the tea and buns came, Rebeka refused to drink. She said that her stomach had not been good lately and she did not want to disturb it. Her father did not even look up at her or ask what could have upset the stomach. If the young woman felt hurt or offended, she did not show. Every time and place was, for them, a battleground. Each knew the other's artillery of destruction and had long learned how to protect themselves from falling rubble and shrapnel.

The question of staying with Martin's father even for a night was out. He had no room to keep guests. The children slept on mats in the sitting room while he and his wife used the inner room. His apology embarrassed Martin so much that he could only look at the floor as his father talked. I remembered him talking about his family, and his father in particular, with such unhappiness, at Mount Meru Hotel when we met for the first time. I understood more clearly his saying, "I sympathize with my father."

There was more laughter at his mother's house where we stayed most of the time. I helped with the preparation of meals while the sister did other things. It was easy for me to adapt to the routine of village life that was the same as where I came from. Sometimes Martin went for walks with his father, ending up at the shop that was also the village bar. I did not go again to say goodbye to the family. Martin did that for both of us to the approval of mother-in- law.

Both of us were relieved when the time came to return to Dar es Salaam.

CHAPTER 9

Six months. Martin's mother had come and taken us to her place and showed the new daughter to her clan. His sister was settling into our house, having found a comfortable life to live without demands. It was time for me to inform my mother and my relations about my new situation. The months of silence must have worried my mother and made Godbless resentful, but I would explain, after all, I had something to show for the silence!

After visiting his parents, I understood why Martin wanted a small and quiet wedding. He had said that he could not handle the noise and demands of family and relations and that he had no money. I had agreed, and left the wedding arrangements in his hands, believing that marriage was a private affair between two people, that the choice was actually ours. A heart full of trust and love had said to him, "You are right, my love."

Martin and I agreed that we should not go together, that I should go first and break the news more softly.

I traveled by bus and had plenty of time to think. I imagined my mother would be happy because her only daughter had been married the proper way, with a husband and a marriage certificate. I hoped she would feel compensated. It was Great Aunt Mai I worried about.

"A girl child is the laughter that brings tears. Truly," she once told me. "When a girl is betrothed, she is made to sit down until her buttocks touch the grass and told: A suitor is good, always good before he lures you into bed and enters you between your legs. A suitor is good before then, because, he hungers for you. His tongue hangs out with desire and he sweats to please you so you can reveal the precious secret you carry with you. And so he should be kept that way until he is given you in marriage by your parents, the way a girl is given to a man, then he can take you into his bed and make you his wife."

Of course I knew Aunt Mai was already outdated. Girls do whatever they like with their men these days. I had asked her, 'And why should it be so, Aunt Mai?'

"Because a man's love is simple and short lived. A man's memory of love is shorter than his index finger, so you must be *his* by having you in *his* house, because then he can neither forget nor abandon you."

I had not believed what Aunt Mai had said, because a man can abandon a woman anytime, especially so when a woman is *his*. Who had not seen that happen? The social laws that forced a man to keep what was his were no longer operative with us. Even that concept of ownership had changed, new meanings, although not clearly defined, had come into force. Still, I was worried because Aunt Mai had been our oasis and could therefore not bear her slightest disappointment. I knew that I had done something she would completely disapprove of, and I needed to know how I would soften her into understanding. Would she understand that love has its own forces that may hit one as in a storm, forces that are intricately linked but are not necessarily tied to the powerful secret between a girl's legs?

All the worries and silly thoughts left me when I saw my mother again. She looked just a bit older, more worn out but as full of vivacity as always. It was good to hear her laugh loudly again, calling on the neighbors to share her happiness. It did not matter whether they heard; it was her way of announcing to the world that her daughter had come.

"Doreen, you have grown up," she said, as she sized me up to see whether I had been taking care of myself well. She did not notice the ring on my finger. After the announcements to the neighbors, we made tea and engaged in small talk. The news related to my 'growing up' was to be kept until after dinner.

But I could not hold the good news until after dinner. I sprang the surprise on them as they started eating, announcing to mother and the whole family that I was married, I had a husband called Martin Patrick, that we lived in Dar es Salaam in a place called Kawe where he had a house of his own. She did not seem impressed at all.

"Martin Patrick? Who is that?" she had asked, after some silence. Her tone sounded like she was asking what that piece of gossip was about and what did it have to do with her! Somehow the flat disinterest in her voice managed to show tension that brought everyone to attention. The light mood of the evening darkened under a cloud.

"Don't tell me those things," she said after another silence. She stopped eating, put the spoon on the plate. I saw her eyes silently fill with tears that trickled down her face. She did not fight them, nor wipe them away. She looked down on her plate, trying to hide her face from the younger boys. I felt a desperate urge to wipe the tears for her. I felt as if I had wronged her somehow, had betrayed her by going away with a man without her knowledge and approval.

"What is it Mother?" I asked in bewilderment.

"Leave me be," she said quietly.

In my mother's house, it was night, the time following dinner, which was saved for talking. The evening meal was eaten only after everything had been done. That way, the time for eating could be extended and the family could talk on and on to while away the night. Night was God's time given to people to rest and find pleasure in each other's company, and so it was the family's social time for laughter and jokes.

It was my mother's established tradition that the cows would be fed and milked, all utensils stored in the house and everyone washed. Washing meant cleaning the legs, hands and face, and except for those who could afford time for pleasure, washing the whole body was done on Sunday. It was my duty for many years to make sure that Alfred and Samson had washed, because left to themselves, they would never do it. After I left home to go to secondary school and later the teachers college, it seemed they grew up and became responsible for themselves, especially after Godbless identified himself apart as a man and not a child anymore.

The culture of eating had changed little since I was a child. Each of us had our own plate and bowl, although we never sat at table. We had no table. Food was apportioned to each of us in the out-kitchen where it was cooked. Apportioning food was my mother's sacred duty, volumes and content being determined by her own knowledge of individual children. So Godbless got the most pieces of meat, larger amounts of sour milk and the largest portion of stew. And of all the children, I got the least. Of all of us, mother got the smallest portion, always making sure that there was some food left in the pot. This, she later gave to Alfred who never refused food, or to Samson, but rarely to me.

We grew up with this tradition which I never questioned until I was in secondary school when I realized that my mother often starved herself so that we could eat! When there was too little food, it was she who did without and I with very little. Then I would eat the *ukoko*, the hard burnt food at the bottom of the pot. This, mother would put on top of a little of the good food. I even liked it, since it tasted like the crusted side of bread, salty and crunchy.

One day in school, close to end of term, one shy and thin girl said, "Sometimes I hate home."

"Why?" several girls chanted.

"Agh, I just hate it," she said again. And the girls started hazarding guesses, pestering her until, in order to refute the strange allegations, spurted, "Its my father. He demands all the meat in the food and only gives some to my brothers and never to us girls. Mother does every thing he says. It is not really the food as such, but, I just *hate* it."

The sharp edges of her statement knocked against the total silence that followed. Then the echo of that declaration opened a flood. The dormitory came awake: "Men have such big stomachs! They are gluttons. They are unkind. So selfish!"

And I asked, "Why did your mother apportion all the meat to your father and none at all to the children?" I was not defending anybody. I just had no example to illustrate a different scenario. I did not want to declare that I had no father, particularly because he was not dead, because like being poor, it was an embarrassment. So the other girls took over the conversation, discussing the matter hotly, each citing varying examples and situations. A window of understanding opened in me, and I knew; oh yes, boys are as *special* as fathers!

That is when I realized that I had supported my mother in upholding a system of favoritism I had been unaware of. I was her accomplice in this process of shaping life, building attitudes and manners even without my knowledge. This realization was so painful it made me cry. I was filled with guilt and shame. How could I not see? All those days I had seen her leave food in the pot when she had hardly eaten enough to fill a baby's stomach, she had gone to bed hungry! All those days. Neither the boys nor I saw this. Sometimes when Alfred did not have enough food and asked for more, mother gave him a little more from her own plate without hesitation. I would hardly have had enough myself, but I never asked for more, because there was no more food. The realization of her sacrifice filled me with love for her, her dedication to our survival felt too huge to repay. I loved her so dearly. What does it take for one to do that? Do all mothers do it for their sons and husbands?

I did not then know about a system that deprived some people for the benefit of others. None of us knew. Mother was just being mother and we were her children. All those years, I never questioned why mother left the house to me to manage and care for others even when I was not the eldest. I supported her as she went around doing her chores, relentlessly, like a black soldier ant, rallying behind her, thinking it is for her. And the boys did only what they could!

When I went home on leave, it was with a sharper consciousness that I observed mother. I loved her for sacrificing her life so that we did not have to beg for food or starve. I loved her, yes, but I also felt hurt. Why should she love the boys more and not care enough for me? Yet, I did not raise those issues, I held my peace, but after that, I took over the role of apportioning food. One day I said, "Let me," and took away the serving spoon from her hand and served food to everybody. I thought she would defend that role as hers not to be usurped. I was surprised at the lack of resistance she showed.

"Take it," she said, casually and simply and settled back on the stool she was sitting on and watched.

My eyes opened further and I looked at her in a new way. Could she have known that it was only a matter of time for me to be ready? Did she know why I took over? Was she waiting for this time to come? Was there an unvoiced code between us that we reacted to subconsciously?

When she let go the role, I could feel that it was her way of showing me that we were partners in this role of nurturing. We were partners at the hearth and she trusted that I would understand the role. When my rations did not follow her pattern, she did not object or even try to influence me. She followed my movements, checking carefully with her eyes. She followed the boys' reactions but did not interfere in my responses. And she ate all the food I put on her plate! She complained that it was too much, but ate all of it finally. Alfred learned to complain less after seeing that mother was not getting involved.

Why then had she done what she did?

After I finished school and became a teacher, I partially took over maintaining the home by sending her money which she acknowledged with few words. "I thank you, God's child." Always she said that. She could not be effusive and give many blessings like

Great Aunt Mai did. This simple denial that she was not responsible for my achievement but that I was God's gift to her always made me want to cry.

My coming home made everyone happy and lifted their mood. My coming was always accompanied by gifts and laughter. Earlier on, mother had even stopped me from getting too close to the hearth, saying that the smoke was not good for me! When did she learn that I too could be spoilt a little? I went in anyway and sat near her and her happiness caressed my heart. After we had tea, talking and laughing together, I opened the big box of presents for everyone that I had brought. She was very happy about the clothes for the boys, finding great happiness in their display. Godbless did not try on the shoes and the outfit, but he beamed. I knew he would do it in his room sometime when no one would be watching and would later tell me how handsome he looked and how the whole village would have to contend with his affluence!

The announcement of my marriage and my mother's tears made Godbless, stand up sharply, flailing his arms, looking in my direction and then my mother's, the words he wanted to say refusing to leave his mouth.

Finally, "*Yaani*, you just decided to go to a husband. You just decided to go! *Yaani*, we don't matter!"

His voice was hoarse with emotion. Alfred and Samson, sensing some kind of danger, ate quickly, looking into their plates, fearing to look up into faces distorted with passions they did not yet know. Their faces did not lose the light that was in their hearts because of the presents. When they left for their room, they giggled with unrestrained happiness.

Mother told Godbless, "Sit down child and rest your soul."

Mother had said it quietly, with resignation, as if after the tears there had come the realization, the inevitable recognition that her partner at the hearth was already a woman who had left her for a man. She told Godbless again, "Truly, sit down and rest your soul."

But Godbless did not sit down. He had little capacity to withstand the onslaught of emotions, especially where those who were close to his heart were concerned. He walked out into the night saying, "I will be right back."

"And where will you go?" Mother said, more to herself, although she was addressing the now absent Godbless. Silence followed her question into the night, then it came back and sat down with us. The eating stopped.

Through force of habit, I cleared the dishes and rinsed them. Abiding by another of my mother's traditions, the dishes would be washed in the morning. "Food must be in the house always," she often said, when we were younger. What woman does not leave some food aside for later or for the following day? She used to say that to me as a way of instruction. I did not see the logic of it because we would be sleeping anyway and the following day would claim its routine of work, food or no food in the house. So, obviously, it must have been for her own reassurance that at no time would she fail to have food in the house for her children. Even the unwashed dishes were a good enough sign.

We did not sit up to wait for Godbless to return. There was no longer any possibility for conversation between Mother and I. We each went to our beds in the room I shared with her as if by legal instruction, the silence between us shouting the emotional confusion both of us were going through. Before we retired into our thoughts, I mumbled in the half darkness, "Martin will come to visit us the day after tomorrow. I will meet him at a place we agreed and bring him home to meet you."

She groaned, as if to shun that reality, to refuse compliance. She said, "It is your affair. You will see what to do."

I did not have the energy or the willingness to beat down the wall she had erected between the reality of my marriage and her life, between Martin's visit and herself. A strange bubble of unhappiness had found residence in my stomach and settled. I was too uncertain of what I had done to make mother so sad she had to cry. I resolved to find time with her the following day, to explain to her that Martin loved me, that I loved him, that he will not turn his back on me. I knew she would understand and forgive me because even as her soul had decided to withdraw into silence, the daemon in me told me that mother had once entered the ring of fire to find love.

Mother was secretive. Her feelings, her thoughts about things that affected her life and the people she loved, were kept somewhere hidden in her being. She said what she chose to say, and only to those she trusted. After I had made her cry, I knew there was no place in that house where I would ask her confidentially how or what I had betrayed. She would not talk, thinking perhaps the boys had not slept.

The house in which we lived started as one room in which mother lived with Godbless for two years before I was born. The other rooms were added on, one after another, so there was no real line to the design, no one room looked like another. The end room on the non- line was the social room where dinner could be eaten and visitors could be invited to sit during the day. It was an open house without room for secrets, and as a girl growing up, my vanity and earthly passions were carefully hidden under lock in a wooden box kept under the bed. The house allowed little privacy; there were no other doors except those that led to the outside, showing clearly that there was no secret life conducted in the house that mother kept from her children, and that any threat to her could only come from outside the three rooms. As Godbless and I grew older, each of us developed the skill to fashion private time from the absences of others. When no one was around, we hurriedly did whatever could not be shared. We knew the necessity of that, Godbless and I, and we respected it. Mother was not part of this understanding. We knew nothing about her, nothing much about her secret life, if she had any, her love or desires. We knew that she worked hard and she slept at night. Her personal life was cocooned within her, well contained and managed.

I have come to an understanding that youth is resilient and malleable, that is why that night, I was sure mother would understand the reason why I had gotten married without her knowledge. But time and the contests with my heart have allowed me to see the frivolity of that assumption. I have often wondered, as stories turn around in my head, whether understanding the meaning of love between a man and a woman enables a mother, to feel any less, the rip at the breast of her girl child going away. Loss is loss, irrespective of the love accompanying it.

I was naïve then to think that my own love for Martin was cure for the sadness mother felt over my leaving home and starting a new life.

CHAPTER 10

Martin's visit became a tender boil that no one wanted to touch. My brother Godbless was friendly, but detached, and when he found time to talk, it was about his responsibilities around the house. He hovered around most of the time, which was uncharacteristic. He pruned banana clusters, fed the fodder to the cows, washed clothes and bullied Alfred and Samson into fetching water enough to fill an irrigation furrow! He did not want to go away, yet he was restless, as if something bothered him. He was keeping himself busy to keep the restlessness in check, behaving like a tethered animal.

"Why don't you rest a bit," I suggested.

"Ha! Soon you will tell me to go to bed," he said with irritation. I let it lie to avoid a senseless quarrel, which it seemed, was the thing he was looking for. As soon as he rinsed the last piece of clothing, he said, "I will be right back," and went away.

He had not returned by dinnertime.

His absence was louder than a scream. I could feel the tension that wrapped around mother fill the room with heat.

She did not ask about him.

I think the announcement that I had branched off, without notice, to start a new life with a man, a total stranger to them, opened a new chapter in our lives. Suddenly the cluster that we were had come loose and the security of the entity came under threat. We were never to be the same people again. Our life was characterized by the cluster instinct, for survival. It was sharpened, lived, like one must breathe in oxygen for the lungs and the brain to work and life regenerated within the body as a continuum. My subsequent visits home have confirmed this to me time and time again. So, like a surprise encounter, that visit marked the turning point in our stories, the parting of the plot lines, the end of the common theme that tied us into a unified entity created from the soul and stubborn tendon that held the will of a woman called Foibe Seko.

It must have had something to do with the way she had carved out her reality from an unfriendly crust. It was a backbreaking task, the fruit of which she guarded like a mother hen, sitting on her young to protect them from the sharp eye of the hawk. She had learned that life could be both kind and cruel.

Mother remained the heartbeat of the cluster; tugging at it with her stubborn, mute resolve. Because it was not anything she could name. These were feelings stored raw, foreign even to her consciousness. These were feelings that gained life under the currency of existence in the struggle for survival as a living organism. Isn't the urge for survival engrained in the living cell? As such, it was part of her life, as breathing is, present, shining through her form, sheer as a layer of translucent spray, imperceptible yet real.

Later, much later, when Martin started changing, running from a softness in him which made him a great lover but not man enough, I came to understand that the story of Godbless and mother, were the twin stories of betrayal. Martin's story added to the same theme. To be born into a world that welcomed him with praise songs because he was the desired one, but with laid out designs to reject him!

Martin's story started with the mother who had a child bride brought into her home because she bore only one son and four girls. The father got two sons from the child-wife. Resentment, jealousy and distrust were cured like leather until it lived between the family members like the family stool that occupied a special place in the home. So there was no real family to bring him and his sisters up, to nest them with love into rounded beings. The older woman, Martin's mother, automatically became the witch vying to kill the young bride's prized sons. The unending fights of the two women, the daughter's acerbic castigation of the father, was the air Martin breathed as a child and as a young man. The web had become the trap for the spider's own eggs, laid and nested in the matrix!

Much later, in my mind, Martin and Godbless rounded out a lesson for me: the stories of motherhood are what marks women and shape their lives. And when these stories are traced within the matrix, they are found to loop the lives of all women's children, female and male.

Martin's mother had her story start with abandonment, Foibe Seko's started with love, naively and abundantly given, cured and wrapped in the seeming warmth of a man's incessant lust, then later betrayed.

Godbless was the first fruit of that love born of youthful naiveté, and the eye opener to knowledge of what it meant to be woman with a womb, for which nature she was held responsible. He, *the child brought on the head.* He was declared enemy before he was born, the artillery for war against him readied within the matrix of social organization.

Mother found out that she *was* different from her brothers. That if they both engaged in sex, nothing would happen to them, because their bodies did not hold and nurture babies, and in so being, nature had exempted them from shame! And then, mother further learnt, that by just being pregnant, her own parents could be *ashamed* of her and because they could not relate to shame, they could chase her away without remorse.

When grandfather ran mother out of the house like a mangy dog and grandmother stood aside and let him do it, she could not imagine that such a thing could happen! She had not found words, in that state of confusion and shock, to appeal to her mother's protection. Her mother had closed herself inside the house and let the father chase his daughter away. It was too hard for mother to accept the terrible truth as she trudged along the path leading to Great Aunt Mai's house, her stomach full of growing Godbless, not so big yet, but made heavier by sadness. She let herself be led by a force she knew was in her because she was alive. Her head was too hot to accommodate thought and reasoning. Even as she entered Great Aunt Mai's house without announcing herself, she could not speak to say what had brought her. She joined the aunt by the fire where she was cooking the evening meal and sat down, tears flowing down her face without restraint. Great Aunt Mai did not ask her why she was crying, what she had come to do or who sent her. She knew the crime and the punishment. She knew too, her structured role in this matrix and so she let her cry. Later, a healthy baby Godbless was born.

And so the tenuous band of umbilical still held the mother and son's souls captive. When Godbless returned that fateful night, mother knew, even without seeing him, that he was drunk. The door was not locked yet so he entered without waking anybody and went straight to his room. The bed moaned desperately as he sat on it adding to the weight of Alfred and Samson, sleeping, one facing north, the other south. The bed was firmly pushed against the wall to achieve stability and to protect the younger boys from falling off as they pushed each other unknowingly in the uneasiness of growing up dreams. Against the opposite wall, on a wooden plank stood two cardboard boxes containing clothes and the boys' knickknacks of every description. They also stood for a table where food for Godbless was left covered by a plate and beside which a small hurricane lamp stood burning with the wick turned low.

"*Where is my father?*" Godbless asked.

It was not a question really. It was a demand for attention, for recognition. A claim to life desired, a voicing of an acutely felt want to be and belong in the order of things. The question was followed by a heavy silence. Godbless must have hung his head between his hands, as was his habit when assailed by emotional stress. He sighed loudly.

"Why?" he asked the night, the shadows, and the sleeping bodies.

That outburst was a shock to me. Where did it come from? From mother's tears the previous evening? Could it have been caused by the announcement of my marriage?

In that small house without room for secrets, that 'why' accompanied by the sigh let out a flood of tension whose currents circulated, slowly, surely, in the silence. The boys sleeping continued to sleep, but the tension enlarged in dimension and hit mother's warm body like a strong current of cold air.

"*What is it?*" she asked.

Godbless did not answer. I sensed my mother's body snapping into tension like a hunted animal sensing danger. She must have *seen* her son in her mind, each of her senses engaging in this task. She listened to him with all her body and the continued silence from Godbless gave birth to something in her, something she *knew* through knowledge of feelings and instincts about those she was intimately bonded to.

Again, Mother asked, "What is it? Why are you not eating."

"I am not hungry," Godbless said after some time.

The words fell heavy and flat on Mother's conscience. She did not even know that he did not eat lunch, but she knew that her children have never had enough to eat in the afternoon, never enough to make Godbless not want dinner. Lunches have always been frugal, resulting from a culture of mother being away in the day and what was available being what I could put together by foraging in the grove.

"*Where is my father?*" Godbless blurted out again.

I lifted my head as if to listen more carefully at what he was bent on saying. The question was fraught with emotion. But it was my mother who reacted with the sharp agility of a mother cat under threat. The thing that was born in her must have matured instantly and sent sharp pin pricks of anxiety to her head.

"*What* is eating you child?" she asked sharply. "Eat your food and go to sleep. I have told you many times to let that liquor be drunk by men who can hold it."

Now she was sitting up in bed, listening. All this tense energy had drawn my mind into its circuit and I was one with Mother as she saw her son clearly in her mind.

At twenty-six, Godbless considered himself a grown man, who sometimes confided in me, "Sister, I am aging and I don't have a girl. Save your brother from perpetual bachelorhood and bring one of your learned friends for me to marry."

"Aah, brother, you have to fall in love at least!" I said.

"Bring her first, I am sure I will love her," he always said, half serious, half in jest. Often, this request was thrown in between the stories we told each other about love and girls, amidst the laughter and jokes.

At his age, he was supposed to at least have a fiancée, a girl people would attach to him and therefore consider him 'normal'. Then when people met him they could say to each other, 'oh, he is engaged to so-and-so's daughter.' Society could then have patience with him for not marrying, finding excuses for him for being alone at a time considered to be beyond the marrying age.

Mother's allusion to his manhood must have touched him where he already felt lacking in terms of social expectations, and so he responded angrily, "Yes, that is what you always tell me. I am not a man! I am not a man! That is all you can tell your son. I am tired. Honestly, I will run away from this place for good."

Sobs punctuated his words, wrung from his chest, rudely, like young, tender shoots uprooted from parched earth. He left the bed, releasing a cry from the bedsprings, walked the few steps to the other room, opened the door and banged it shut.

He was swallowed by the night.

"Godbless! Child, where are you going?"

The fright in Mother's voice, sharp like a knife blade, sliced the night. It must have opened her excited mind to wild thoughts. She left the bed with a sprint uncommon in her age, and opening the back door, she too plunged into the night. I heard her ask, "What is this evil thing coming to my house? What does it want from me?"

Her voice had a peculiar character. It was heavy, without resonance.

I knew mother was trembling, her limbs shaking so much it was a miracle they did not collapse. That is how she lived fear, through trembling, the intensity of that force subjecting the frame of her body to a shakeup, dissolving the elegance, the command in her that had made us fear her all the years of our childhood.

· I sensed that she was looking everywhere for Godbless, behind the house, among the banana plants, in the open courtyard where she must have pushed darkness aside with her hands as if it were tangible mass.

"Child, why do you make me suffer so?"

The night in which she wandered without direction was infested with shadows. Fear held her tightly and clung to her heart's delicate fiber. Her mind must have acted like a camera, seeing and registering without question or comment as she moved silently in the dark. Never should one call a beloved's name in the dark where bad spirits reign. Never.

After a while, I heard her leave the shadows and enter the courtyard again. I sensed and felt with her the low fire in her stomach opening up her whole body to an invasion of a strange weakness. Something in her very center must have dissolved. She tripped over a corncob and fell.

I heard a deep groan. It moved me from the bed where I sat, folded into a knob of tension, resolutely having refused to be drawn into the net of their quarrel. I ran out, following the sound.

Mother would not rise from where she lay.

"Mama, mama, please don't die. Please ma, please don't die!" Godbless was saying, emerging from the dark. I reached mother almost at the same time as he, both of us reaching for her where she lay. My heart was beating through my ears. We extended our hands towards her in a kind of plea. We were the desperate ones, the ones needing her. Drops of warm water fell on Mother's face as both me and Godbless tried to lift her, both of us crying silently. We supported each other into the house whose warmth enfolded our bodies like a blanket. Godbless' ghastly cheeks and chin were wet.

Once inside, Mother pointed a finger towards her bed. She did not show fear on her face, just exhaustion. She looked drained. Godbless and Mother did not talk to each other. A force greater than their immediate passion parted them, like a ripe fruit drops off the branch of a parent tree due to its own inner volition. I supported mother to her bed and Godbless went to his.

We heard him blow his nose roughly.

"God, tell me what this child wants," Mother said, after getting into bed, hugging the blanket to her body.

I got into bed again, feeling cold all over. I wanted to appeal to Mother to sleep, to reserve her questions for daylight when her emotions would have settled and her mind could be called to reason. Discourse with God must be engaged in with a sober mind lest the argument turn against her. But her heart had not released Godbless yet, and I did not yet exist with her in that room, so realizing this, I kept quiet. I sought for warmth in the blanket and wondered whether Mother knew of her son's most intimate desires. But even if she did, would she help him realize them?

In the twin stories, twined like vine upon a tree, the common plot line had ended. The inevitable individual struggle, independent and personal, had commenced. I once heard a plaintive song on the radio saying;

> *'My heart is a weight of love in my chest*
> *My heart is burdened with love yoked*
> *with the twin sides of desire.*
> *It cries for want of freedom*
> *from such delicate bonds...'*

The song came to mind as I imagined my mother feeling that way about her son, acutely loving him, wanting to ensure his happiness by holding him to her, wanting to protect him from harm, but being compelled to let him go his way.

Even today, when my mother is on my mind, the spirit of Godbless hovers nearby, automatically, as if waiting for me to trace the story of this love to the end. And always, I behave like the child who thinks closing the eyes tight puts off an impending danger. Everything will be alright, the mind tells the heart, which knows that mother's tears brought a new sub plot into the story.

When I stayed with Great Aunt Mai for some time during my holidays in secondary school, she told me how mother lost confidence in her own parents when she was run out of the home.

"Your mother has lived with anger since then. She must learn forgiveness. She believed in her parents, without reserve, like all children believe in the benevolence of the mother. But you know, the thing that eats parts of itself looks for its own annihilation! That is what happened. Yes, we dropped her on hard rock and broke her bones!"

Great Aunt Mai said many things to me after she considered me grown up enough to understand. In any case, I asked too many questions, craved too much for answers.

She said, "Your mother's pregnancy was not noticed early enough. She did not know the stomach would grow!"

"What would have happened if it was known?"

"I could have taken her before she was chased away. Her mother was too frightened by the time all came to light. Bad things could happen to a girl who becomes pregnant before she is given off to a man in marriage," Great Aunt Mai said.

And so the scorn that washed on her for the rest of the pregnancy had started from her family. Her father had become so angry, he threatened to throw her in the forest for the hyenas to eat!

"She was too young to understand tradition," Aunt Mai had said.

But what was the root of this tradition?

I lived with Great Aunt Mai's statement throughout my youth, wondering about society and tradition. How could it acknowledge the nature that ensured its survival as crime? How could it gang up against its own kind, suddenly finding worthlessness where before there was pride and ownership? What caused that shift of value?

Thinking about all this, I really came to understand that Godbless was the child that *must* be Mother's. Not me or even the other boys who followed. So, how could Godbless want to leave her, ever, when they all thought he was a creature not worthy of life?

I lay in bed, my body still cold, and channeled into the current of thoughts between mother and Godbless. I marveled at this strange knot of mother-love. Is it in every woman? Does it start at every birth and grow with every sharing and relating between mother and child, coalescing as a stone is formed from dust and the forces of environment, into a relationship? Relationships do turn around and grow on people, growing in them and around them. They grow by them, like partners, attaining life and character, breathing in definite pulses like a third entity. The eye of my senses could see this between Godbless and mother. I had always been able to feel it, but it was nameless in my mind. When we were growing up, mother was always more sensitive to his needs, his hurts and cries. "What is wrong with the child?" mother would enquire at the slightest raising of the child's voice. "Why is the child crying," she would ask me, her face reflecting the inner disturbance. I was younger, but I did not feel young, could not feel young. I automatically became older the moment my legs and hands were tempered to serve. She would be concerned if he did not eat well. When Godbless was sad, mother would do everything to cheer him up. I saw that, felt the inner tension instinctively, and accepted it as normal.

Then Godbless grew up and apart from her and I could see how the chasm shimmered with emotional tension between the two. When mother said to Godbless, "Sit down and rest your soul, truly," I could feel the desire to shield her man - child from pain come to flower in her heart.

"*What is this he seeks?*" she asked again in the dark. Her voice was querulous and demanding.

From the other room, Godbless said, "I don't know. I ___." Hiccups that jammed his speech seized him. "I *hic* almost kill- *hic*, killed you."

"Drink some water and rest. Rest. Quiet down and leave all to God," Mother said, tiredly, quietly.

"Now my mother, listen, *hic* to me. I am saying this, if only *hic* he came once. Only once. If he could call to me 'son' and I would answer, 'yes my father.' Then he would hold my hand *hic, hic* and sit with me and tell me something, things that fathers tell their sons. If only he *hic*, if only *hic, hic*, could even ask me 'are you *hic* taking care of your mother well? Only that. Is that a big thing to ask from him? Eh, is it?"

Godbless started to sob again, quietly.

Mother said, more to herself than Godbless, "Do not trouble your heart, son. Truly, do not wring your spirit like wet cloth. What can you get from him now?"

Hearing that, I thought, what do people do with sustained longing and desire?

These questions have not stopped tracking my path. It is as though the answers are a debt I owe someone. My brother Godbless, Zima, and then Martin and finally Joseph. How long can one sustain thirst before it shrinks the inside into hate, or worse?

Time has allowed me to see that for Godbless and mother, there was in them a passion not at all veined in filial love. It was the violence bred from unvested passions for the one man both of them loved desperately. For mother, it was the loss of beauty, the curtailing of her spirit's search for what could have fulfilled the nature of her spirituality. Godbless was locked out in the cold, without identity, denied acceptability by those who defined his place. This unnamed passion they had harbored for so long was directed not to the man, but to themselves, for being so weak and helpless against the power of this man who so easily abandoned them, abandoned all of us without paying, in any way.

CHAPTER 11

A legend spoke of my mother's love for one man, one man only. She refused, after the betrayal, to utter a word about it. She had lived it, she explained quietly to those who asked her about it, as if the story were tonic to weak hearts. "What did people want from me?" she always asked in bewilderment.

Great Aunt Mai refused to be involved. "Leave me alone, child!" She dismissed me with great impatience. "Is your head sick, that you want to fill it with nonsense that has had no direction at all? Go. Leave your mother's wound be. Go."

And so it was that I relied on stories narrated by people, over time, in order to know what had happened to my mother as a young girl. In order to understand why our life was as it was.

It was said that Sebastian Shose was a seducer. Women said that he never tired until his love wish was attained. He was a man sought after by many girls, and because of this, all kinds of behaviors were attributed to him. He was a promiscuous person, shameless in his pursuits, some girls said. He was morally corrupt, a shame to the upright family from which he came, the women said. He loved my mother when she was fifteen, and he, ten years older, only a year married, with an infant child. All the three, Mother, Sebastian and his wife were the products of the village primary school, having graduated and walked the dead end street of their dreams. All had fallen into the order of village life. They cultivated the fields according to the dictates of the season, planted, weeded and harvested. The men, as well as the women, went through this known routine, all their lives. Women did more; they cut fodder for the cows, collected firewood and fetched water, looked after the children, catered to the husbands and the homes. On Sunday, the children went to Sunday school, men and women, in their best outfits, went to church.

It was said by his teachers that Sebastian was an intelligent student, very energetic but without discipline. He loved play and he enticed others, the weak ones who could not say no to his face, to play with him, knowing very well that when the tests came, he would pass while the others, failed. His teachers punished him for that unruliness, but other children loved to be identified with him, so he was never short of friends to play with. They said Sebastian was too big and uncontainable for the village, they hoped he would pass and go to other schools where he would find his match. He did not get a chance to get into secondary school. "Chances for rural schools were few or not there at all," his teacher told his father, a well placed church elder, and an influential man.

Sebastian became an apprentice to the best carpenter in the village, making furniture, chairs and tables for ordinary homes. In village terms, he was considered a young man with a future. He earned money, regularly. The job tamed him a bit, as he had no time to relax except on Sundays. His father chose a wife for him from a nice family in the village. Sebastian was married young in order to prevent what his father thought was an incurable and embarrassing waywardness.

Nobody hides from another in the village, as all places are communal- the stream where people fetch water, the grinding mill where they take grain to grind into flour, the shop where daily purchases are obtained, the church... Sebastian sent love messages through Foibe's friends when she herself became too illusive to get. Work had stayed his energies, had made him calmer, but marriage had not been able to reign the need for his perpetual search for love and being loved. Foibe was a hard working girl who hardly tarried anywhere to gossip with other girls or to play. Her father was strict. She got the letters, ignored them for a year, before she gave in, partly due to pressure from her friends, who thought that perhaps Sebastian had finally fallen in love. Why would he be persistent on just the one girl for a whole year? But her heart had also softened to his persistence. Her friends kept the love a secret, providing alibis for her absences and denying any leading questions asked, until the pregnancy claimed its own publicity. When the rumors started going around the village, Great Aunt Mai would shout in frustration saying that only a young man with a bad head would scout the river looking for trysting places! He needed a good spanking, she would say, shaking her head as if wishing she were Sebastian's mother.

"And the girl, so young...," the unsaid opinion hung ominously around us like taboo for years. But then we were too young to understand. When I started comprehending pieces of that legend, I imagined how my mother bubbled with energy and naiveté as she took to being loved like a child takes to a mother's breast. Looking into the lover's eyes must have been like looking into a pond of clear water. It must have drawn her in, and she, diving and swimming with the ease of one so young and indulged with attention. After it had all happened and the scandal had broken, mother's friends came to tell how she had finally agreed to meet him at a place by the river, hidden from public view by bushes of flowering shrubs. But by then, Foibe had been captured, totally.

The man had been full of laughter and sweet words. One year had ripened him with desire. The girl was so taken, so intoxicated with everything which happened. She was a virgin. It was the first time she had seen an erection, and not knowing what was done with it, she covered her face with her hands and waited for the next action. He was gentle. She was tense with curiosity and expectation. He caressed her body. She felt different, pleasant sensations washed over her whole body. He talked to her softly, saying things she did not hear, did not comprehend. He knew the ritual, was experienced, and so he put her at ease, touching her tenderly everywhere, stroking her nipples, holding her so close to his body. When he said, hoarsely, "It will hurt, just a bit," a fire swept through her body, burning all the way to her toes.

That is how the road into her body was paved, harshly, so that she could not tell if what she felt was pain or pleasure. Distantly, there was an awareness outside her body, tangled in sweet - sour feeling, intricately enjoined with the man on top of her. She knew, somehow, that the fire between her legs would not always be there, that the sharp tenderness that had invaded her body would ease.

After the first time, love became a personal thing, unrelated to anything else outside them. He helped her learn to touch him too, taking her hand and directing it to places on his body. Her body woke up to the meaning of pleasure. Then, everything she felt found embodiment in Sebastian. She called him just S. Her happiness was where S was, it was what they did together, what they planned together, in the laughter they shared. She saw love for S in the rising sun in the early morning when she woke up, earlier than anyone else in the house, to fetch water and prepare breakfast. She saw it in the wind as she felt the cool air brush against her face, in the ruffling of leaves, in the moo-ing of cows. She felt him, smelled him, and heard his whispers in every sound and expression that affirmed life. He lived with his wife and child, so she did not ache too much with desire to reach him because she felt him alive inside her. She learned to talk to him, in her mind, telling him stories that he listened to quietly, like he always did when they were physically together. In that way, she lived with him. S. had married her without marrying her; he had bonded her to him without bonding himself to her. And because the man had found a seat in her heart, she found peace in the mystery and depth of her love for him.

The man could not keep away from her. He sought her all the time, following her to places every time he got the chance. His work suffered, he lost all sense of caution. They got trapped, both of them, in that uncontainable magic. In this they became one soul, their love a solid wall around them. Their hearts started tracking the footprints of a timeless dance, following the pattern of a ritual enacted within the consuming ring of fire.

She learned to enjoy the simple miracle of their bodies. She hungered for the un-namable addictiveness attained from the mating game. Always, after feasting they rested, lying on soft grass as the light of the sun turned a faint red. Then came the twilight silence that filled the place with peace, enveloping their tired bodies with sleep. They slept the sleep of the innocent, their bodies tangled, not having separated, unconsciously not wanting to attain individual physicality. Their innocence was covered, warmly, by the distinct mood of the river - the big old trees hanging towards the river as if in supplication to a god; the *ssshh* sound the branches made in the slightest wind; the birds, chirping nervously and moving from branch to branch as in the uncontrolled excitement seen in children. It was all subtly seductive, almost surreal. The river's chuckling noises in its passage downstream sounded like music. Nothing would be wrong with them, she always thought, not as long as the man loved her and the river continued to sing its song in its perpetual journey.

That is how months came and went quickly as if herded on by an unknown hand.

Sebastian, being older and more experienced already knew she was pregnant. He did not tell her. He could not risk stemming out the life sustaining tenderness that seemed to rise from the very pores of the young girl's soft body to meet his want. What he felt for this girl was new to his experience, his mind, new to his body. It had turned the dull, routine world of his life into a scented, beautiful flower. He felt energetic and friendly to everyone.

Sebastian explained away the tiredness that she said she felt. "You work too hard, my love. You wake up too early," he said to her, the concern in his eyes convincing her about the truth of what he said. He brought, to the trysting places, all kinds of fruits to tease the lack of appetite she complained about. Always, after sex, still tangled, he held her very, very close to him, as if he was afraid that during sleep she would shrink and turn into a leaf and float away downstream, apart from him.

What would he do without their trysting? What would life be without her who had become his dream?

He became infinitely softer with her, so much more endearing.

The worry in him was starting to concern her, but she did not understand its cause. When he doted on her, she protested. "You spoil me too much," chuckling throatily like the river water.

"Don't leave me please. Do not leave me ever," he pleaded.

"I will never leave you. I will always love you," she affirmed.

She saw fear in his eyes, but he camouflaged it saying it was the concern for the safety of their love. That was all he was worried about, he assured her.

One day, Sebastian's father summoned him. He reprimanded Sebastian for rampaging in other people's houses like a hungry and greedy bull. No man worth of respect turns his back on the home! The church elder was angry, the integrity of his family was at stake. Sebastian was shocked. How did his father know? It meant the wife knew too.

"I am a grown man, father. I am not a little boy," Sebastian said, his heart pounding in fear, his temples pulsing.

"You have a wife. Your marriage was blessed in the house of God. I should not hear of you being the devil's servant again," his father said.

People say that Sebastian pleaded with his father. "I love her, father. I love her more than anybody or anything in the world," he said, in desperation. "My life will be empty without her."

"Love?" the father almost screamed. "What love? How can any feeling for a woman surpass the obligation to follow the way of the Lord? The bible teaches us that those who fear God walk the narrow road. My son, you are lusting for her, and that is a shame, a great sin. The demon has you by the throat."

His father was incensed, trembling with fear. He clutched at his chest, his heart was giving in to rising pressure. "Oh God, I ask from you the strength to fight the power of Satan. Deliver my son from the demon's grip, oh Lord," he prayed passionately.

"We should pray, my son, so that we are not all killed by it."

His father fell on his knees and started praying. Sebastian went out and left his father on his knees. The village regarded Sebastian as heartless, a man without respect for his father, one deserving to be cursed. It was said that the young girl had bewitched him, had made him loose all sense of who he was.

Trysting by the river was marred by new fears. Their laughter was tamed. Sebastian worried: Who lay in wait beyond the flowering shrubs, peeping, planning to catch them? What wrong had they done? Why should his father be so concerned?

Sebastian knew that his lover was too young to understand the margins of wrong and right in loving and being loved, so he did not tell her about the encounter with his father for some time. He could not explain how his father had known about them. He could not explain to her the implications behind his father's knowledge of their love.

When he came to tell her what was already becoming a scandal in the village, she had asked, "Is what we are doing a very bad thing?"

His throat constricted with pain and guilt. She is too young, too young and beautiful and innocent, he thought desperately. He felt responsible for her state, of which she was yet ignorant. What was he to do? Where could he take her? The village felt small and confining.

The village talked, not about the love, but about the state of the church elder and his son. "Truly, the son is going to kill his father," people said.

Sebastian's wife acted as the best daughter-in-law in their time of test. She cared for the old parents without showing any grudge to the husband. They were her parents too, she told people. God will be on her side and help her in laws to pull through this crisis. The village praised her, lavishing her with indulgences. "She is exemplary! A wife to be proud of," they said.

One day, Foibe's mother brought two women friends home to visit. They summoned Foibe and talked to her about how girls are supposed to live a chaste and Christian life until they are given to a husband in marriage. All girls who are brought up well do not repay their parents with unkindness by behaving like mangy dogs!

"Have you been sleeping with any man?" they asked. Her mother let the other women talk, watching over them like a teacher supervising an exam. Foibe resented it, but remained silent. "Do you know a man called Sebastian Shose?"

Foibe's heart skipped a beat. They too know! She realized. That fact changed things, changed her mood and her stance to the women. "I love him," her heart screamed silently. She looked directly in the eyes of the woman who had asked the question, stared at her, then the others, without saying a word. But really, no word would have matched the defiance in her eyes!

That is when the women got angry and spanked her thoroughly. They used the blunt and curved end of *kyinndo*, the banana peeling knife, warmed under hot ash, to hold the skin between the knife and the thumb, as if to peel it away from the flesh. It burned and scraped her skin, the burnt lines on the flesh where the knife held the skin rising immediately. Foibe cried, like a baby. They told her how this treatment will teach her to close her thighs, how it will be good medicine for her shameless, wanton love for sex.

The fresh scars all over his lover's thighs shocked Sebastian. "Oh God, Oh God," he said, his eyes watering, the tears dropping on the lacerations. He knew that he could not soothe her pain no matter what he did or said. She had suffered alone, without him to defend her, to put up a case of her innocence. They cried together, and sat for hours without speech. There was no place for them to go. The place behind the flowering shrubs was almost their home, but they could not sleep there all night, every day, they could not live there. Their trysting gradually withered like a plant denied water, but the curtailed passion remained with them, reducing the man to a state of somber and detached quietness. The girl carried sadness like a tarnished sheen underneath the youthfulness of her face.

CHAPTER 12

Did mother understand the cause of the sadness she had carried in her heart on the long road of her life?

The man who sought her love could not keep away. He continued to plead, tracking her with the same persistence as when he courted her. What would his life be without her love? What was he to do with the fire that ravaged his body? He could not stop thinking of her. Her presence in his life had meant more than he could ever know: her quiet voice, the softness of her body, the innocence of her thoughts, her smile, their discussion of everything that happened to both of them...her face stood before his eyes like an apparition. What could he do?

He did not care what anyone said, not his father, not the wife and not all the people in the village. His heart was withering and his body burning, dying the slow death of thirst for her.

But his lover was under guard. She never went anywhere alone without her younger sister.

When she was finally able to escape and meet him, it was to tell him that something moved inside of her. She did not know what it was.

He held her carefully, they made love tenderly. The suppressed passion came aflame like a bush fire fanned by an ominous wind.

"I wish I could take you away from the village. I wish there was a place for us to go to," he said, as if pleading.

"Why do you want to go away?" she asked. "It will all pass. People will talk and then they will forget. It is going to be okay," she comforted him.

He did not explain about the thing that moved inside of her. A fear tugged at his throat so that he did not know how to say it. What was he to do? That question went round and round in his mind, loosely, like the movement of a broken wheel. He held on to her, enfolding his arms around her as if she was his life jacket in a deep and threatening sea. But it was her he saw sinking, without help from him. All he felt, as he embraced her tenderly, was helplessness and desperation.

Those were the embraces that became the warm shawl that eased her body of the cold and insinuating scorn. His love, the energy tonic she drank to wake up in the morning, to sleep at night, and find enough appetite to eat so that the love child growing in her womb was nourished.

Everything changed when her mother found out that she was pregnant. Her world turned over so quickly she was dizzied by events. When she went to live with Aunt Mai, the trysting ceased. She was too weighed with sadness to walk to the river.

When Godbless was born, the lover contacted her again through her friend Teki, but she was no longer partial to their love. Every move the lovers made found its way in the gossip channels of the village. And again, their efforts to meet were stopped.

Godbless was six months when they finally met again. The man looked older and sullen. He held her warmly, but the fire that had ringed them had waned to a weak flame. The pools of his eyes were too empty and sunless, without the rebellion of dreams. Mother, still young, but almost a year separated from love, with a boy child, the experience of pain had colored everything a different hue. The shrubs which had been their nest against the world, looked threatening. The ease to laugh, to talk, to touch, felt rheumatic. A certain panic and desperation for the run away magic held her, her heart refusing to take loss as a bargain for social acceptance. But, she did not know what to do to reclaim laughter.

That was my mother's story, gathered from people's words and gestures, from the silent language of her eyes. A story strung together, like a necklace of gemstones in different colors.

I am amazed at how our story lines join, all the time, my mother's and mine, Godbless' and Martin's. The places, the meetings, and the soul's mirror flashing back to us reflections of bodies without skin, without shadows. Hearts pumping blood, pulsating veins, vital forces ... Life so tender.

Lovers are magicians and loving is a ritual dance. When the rhythm eludes the dancer, when the lover's sorcery cannot hold the heart in the ritual dance, absence becomes the seat of longing.

Is that why it hurts too much? Is that why nothing has soothed Mother's pain of that lost love?

My mother was too young to fathom the puzzle. She must have reasoned that they needed time, too much had happened. My mother was always a believer in anything or anyone she loved. When she tried again, nocturnal life possessed their favorite time and place, pushing them away, alienating them from one another. Silence replaced conversation. When they found nothing to talk about, he asked, "Does he look a lot like me?

Mother had smiled faintly, then said, "Yes."

"I desire to see him."

"You will have to come to Aunt Mai's house to hold him," she said.

"How do I do that? It is not even your father's house. And what will your Aunt do to you, after what your father did to you and your mother?

"You will come. You will say, *hodi*. Someone will respond and ask you to come into the house. Then you will enter and say that you have come to see your child, that is accepted, isn't it?"

"No, no. I cannot do that. Your uncle will certainly kill me or call the elders on me, then what will happen to you?"

The young mother was silent, thinking: what defeats love so easily? Why doesn't he fight to the end? The questions came with the realization: they have no freedom, so there is no end to fight for! The desperation for magic released its prisoner and she felt completely empty, defeated. The emotional link to the man unlocked and gave way somewhere in her. She knew, instinctively, as she lay beside him looking at the early night stars before they parted and each went home, that her young son would not have him as father. He was not willing to be one; he was already trapped and tamed.

She resolved then, in her mind, to be both father and mother to her child, and to all her children. That is why we never saw a man around our home, one to help her feed or clothe or care for us. It was either Sebastian or there was no father to her children. That is also why we never knew we were poor because she shielded us from feeling poor.

The lovers must yet have attempted to have sex again because I was born of the same father. Was she trying to snatch the magic back from the dusky sky, with the stars already dotting the night dome?

I reach out for that story now in greater understanding. It was not anger that had sustained her resolve as I had earlier thought. It was a necessary act of courage, for such a young woman, to come face to face with abandonment! What would have happened to her if she had returned to her father's home? What would a life long ridicule and scorn do to her being, especially if no man came to rescue her from it in time by marrying her?

Mother had already tasted the poison of social cruelty and knew that she could brace herself for a war only when she lived alone. That must be when she readied herself for the life long struggle with her daemon. The presence in her that would push her on to defy the rules set by the male order against her femaleness. But female she loved being, so she learned to live in the world of men, so that the death of passion for the one love of her life left only a thin layer of ash upon her heart. Her spirit was of a nature too wild to tame and strap into conformity.

And so the messenger of her fate was Great Aunt Mai, the woman who helped Mother cross the shaky bridge to independence. As her custodian through a loop - hole of the same social code that chased her away from her parent's home, Aunt Mai, tended motherhood in my mother. She knew the psychological harm that came to girls treated like that, she watched out for the signs, averting them tactfully, indulging the young girl like a doctor who knows her patient well. She knew what to say, and what to do when mother, for example, refused to take a bath for over a week; when she did not greet anyone, sometimes including Aunt Mai or Uncle Simbo; when she cried uncontrollably and could not be consoled for a whole day; when she did not want to hold and breastfeed her baby. It was Aunt Mai's duty to nurse the victim. Her duty to have her in her house until she delivered the child, to have her after the child was born, until the father, if willing, took his daughter back. Tradition allowed it. After a father's anger was spent, he could want his daughter back home. Aunt Mai knew, somehow, that mother would not return .

She told me, "When love vacates a person's heart, one can know. God's light, which normally shines in the eyes goes out and they become hollow like an abandoned house. Power does not touch emptiness. Power cannot *affect* emptiness. Your mother did not care anymore about whatever her father and mother did to her. I was afraid she would run away if she was forced to return home."

"What did you do then?"

"When her father said she could go back home, inviting the men and women of the clan to witness her return, I went alone and told them that Foibe was mine. She is my daughter now. I need her to make my hearth warm by kindling the fire in the morning. The crying of the grandson has brought life back into the house, and even my husband has learned to blabber like the child does. How can you want Foibe now and wish me and my man death?"

So they could not refuse Great Aunt Mai that request. Their daughter had already lived with her for two years. They also knew that it was almost as if Aunt Mai had no child. Uncle Simbo was fond of saying that their one child, a boy, went to school and did so well that white people took him to their place and gave him all the education available in the world. They also married him to a woman of their tribe and gave him a job. Although they were well provided for, Aunt Mai would say, money could never kindle the fire in the hearth when it is cold. Money could not greet or scratch a mother or father's back, tired from bending in the field. So luck was with her as she used the rules of the same game to gain a daughter and a grandson.

Aunt Mai knew too, that asking Mother to return home would justify a ritual whose social code cushioned her parents from taking blame for their action. She said that even if my grandfather had taken a sword and cut my mother's throat, social ethic would have attributed it to hot anger, caused by extreme shame and would have found forgiveness for that action.

"That is just how it is," Aunt Mai had said. "A child who comes carried on the head is never liked, especially when it is a boy. And the woman who brings such a child to the home is nothing but a curse."

Great Aunt Mai explained that strange philosophy of children who come into the world carried on the head, as those born before their mothers have a husband. They were feared that they would, in time, come to usurp property belonging to the rightful children. It was feared that they could even kill the rightful children in order to protect their position. My mother must have come to know, having brought a boy child on her head, from a lover trapped into submission by forces of social laws, that she had to channel her own course in life. She knew that the life of her child would always be a point of reference, a reason for misfortunes befalling the family, an illustration for the evil brought on the family by those who come carried on the head!

Aunt Mai had said to Mother, "A woman becomes a social orphan just by being woman. It is not even your father's fault."

By the time I grew up to recognize things, Mother was a woman who had reached a realization that her strength, and the basis for her life and happiness, was in the value of her labor. She nurtured us to believe the same. She had learned also that a woman's sexual life must be hers, to own and control, utterly. So, the men she slept with were not, *could not*, be part of our life. That is how she managed it, by keeping the strictest distance between them and the center of her life. I never knew her men, never saw them. I never saw any expression of love between her and a man. We could never tell if there was a lover among those who visited. Love was never openly expressed, even between her and ourselves. When Alfred was born and then two years later, Samson, they were welcome additions to our home. We never talked about their parentage. It would be unbecoming, an act of extreme indiscipline. Much later, of course, I understood that the pain and bruises of us growing up were treated by mother with the seasoned knowledge of motherhood that was never the same with Godbless. No wonder I left home so easily when love called at my door. The tie between mother and I was of another kind, of another intensity. I could tear the bond between us without qualms, following the trail of love like a sleepwalker.

"You are your own father now. Go your way and let the man go," she had mumbled to Godbless that night. Oh, yes, it was not anger she had used to keep her son away from the father who did not want him. Both wanted to belong to a world, a friendly world. Hers, the one she had created, and the son's, the social order that defined a definite place for a man, but in which he felt excluded. She just had to fight the son's desire with hers. It was a fierce battle for the reclamation of place and love denied. And so her son would have to be the seminal *seed*, the beginning of a line, *his* line, tied to her *alone*, outside her father who chased her away like a mangy dog, and the lover who abandoned her love.

Godbless got a piece of land, a *place*, his own soil and rocks and trees. A place where he could settle, where the spirits which love life more than systems would be warm and friendly. A place. His own piece of earth that would finally accept his bones.

CHAPTER 13

Martin came home. Mother stayed inside the house. The greetings came at the same time from all the boys, Godbless, Alfred and Samson, standing in the middle of the compound. They saw us approach and waited, trying hard to smile and hide their doubts. Samson looked up at Godbless for guidance on what to do. I laughed. They looked comic, although well dressed. Alfred and Samson wore the clothes I had brought them. They must have looked brand new to Martin who smiled at the lined up young people who made him look like a president coming to inspect the armed forces. The charm in his smile must have dissolved all suspicion about the stranger coming to claim space among them.

It felt like the expended emotions of the night had washed all of us, leaving us clean and ready to receive Martin. The boys were respectful and shy, and mother, in her Sunday dress, was very polite and warm when she came out from the inner room to greet the guest. After mother's greeting, Godbless gave Martin a strong handshake, addressing him as brother-in-law and welcoming him to the family.

Godbless laughed and cracked jokes about village life. "We need a young woman in this house now that you have taken my sister and friend away with you. I am also thinking of marrying," he told Martin, almost immediately after he sat down. Martin encouraged him by promising to buy the wedding suit as his present.

We were surprised, mother and I, by the declaration, and the way he made it, in public before a guest just arrived, as if to discourage comment or demand for elaboration. Nevertheless, mother was happy to hear Godbless announce his intention to marry. She laughed mirthfully and said, "Oh, yes. A man does not live alone forever. God did not create him so."

Godbless served the drinks I had bought. Aunt Mai was late but mother apologized for her, explaining how busy and forgetful Aunt Mai could be. "Aunt Mai is my mother. Yes..." mother said, trailing off that addition she must have thought unnecessary for Martin to know. Just then we heard, "*Na ma mbe.* Foibe, are you in?"

"Come into the house," mother responded loudly from where she sat. Godbless relieved Aunt Mai of the can containing local brew which she carried on her head as she complained, almost automatically, that her neck was giving in.

Aunt Mai came with her husband, who carried his characteristic walking stick, leaning on it every time he stood still. They were immediately welcomed and introduced by the master of ceremony, Godbless, who served each of them a beer, keeping the *mbege* for the rituals. Uncle Simbo, Mai's quiet husband extended his glass of beer to Martin as a sign of welcome and Martin sipped from it and returned it to him.

The conversation was light and mirthful. We talked about many things, about the village and the people, asking Martin if he saw any differences with his own village, about national events that had been heard on the radio, about births and deaths, family and friends, each subject flowing into the conversation in its turn, carried by the mood of the speaker and the way each responded to the discussion. Alfred and Samson soon got bored and ran outside to play and show off their clothes to the neighbors. They would explain in detail about the new guest and what, from their perspective, it all meant to the family, which most likely would be the possibility of more clothes and shoes.

Then Great Aunt Mai said, "Child of God, bring me the *mbege* in a calabash." Godbless brought the liquor and Aunt Mai stood up and started calling upon the ancestors, each by name, the women first, the bearers of children, those who nurse them from their own breasts from when they are born. She greeted them, telling them what was happening, appealing to them not to get angry with her, because if they did, they would have followed the example of the woman who denies a child her breast. She asked them to share the food this child called Doreen has cooked and brought before them so that they too could know that she has grown up like all women do. She spilled the mbege on the ground. She appealed to them to come eat and bless the child called Doreen so she could be a woman like they all were, so that she could have children like they all did, so that her hearth would always be warm and the pot of milk will always have milk. And she drank from what was left in the calabash and told mother, "Come Foibe, take this calabash from me. Drink with your mothers and your mother's mothers. Drink until you are full so that they can know you are not mean and a miserly. So that they can know you are not barren and your children are not barren. Come drink with your mothers." And mother received the calabash of mbege, drank from it and continued to hold it. And Godbless, as if on cue brought another calabash and handed it to Aunt Mai.

She addressed the male ancestors as fathers of the *mbengye*, the way to the homestead, the warriors guards of the homes. They had already seen who has come through the entrance to call on the house and they knew that the guest - child has come in peace and humility. The guest - child was looking for a home and asking them to look upon him and welcome him, ask him in. She asked for their forgiveness because the guest- child had come into men's houses alone, as if he had no people, as if he was an orphan, but he is a child, and children do not know that they have no mouth to speak with men. And she spilt the mbege again. A lot of it, more than she gave the women. And she gave the calabash to Uncle Simbo who welcomed her as though she had just arrived home from a long journey. He took the calabash from her and drank from it and then gave it to Martin and said, "Receive this from me child and drink."

Martin took the calabash and drank from it and surprising me and everybody else, he spilt the mbege as he had seen Aunt Mai do and spoke in his language to the ancestors. And after he was done, he went to mother and bent on one knee and offered her the calabash to drink from it. We were all quiet, the whole time, so that it felt very much like praying. Mother drank from the calabash and returned it to Martin who then did the same thing to great Aunt Mai and then finally to Uncle Simbo who drank and remained with the calabash and said simply, "You are a man, my child."

The rituals, the food, the drinks, the friendship, it felt truly like a celebration. It made me so proud of my family and I was so happy that Martin stepped right into the magnetic field of the happy mood and frolicked in it.

I remember that day with warmth. That was really the day I was given to Martin in marriage, by my people, the living and the dead.

That was the day the ancestors accepted him because he presented himself to them, argued his own case for coming without elders, using his own tongue, saying that the language of the spirit cut across tribes. I respected him so much. Even now, in spite of everything that has happened to us, memories of the past are like a granary of corn I feed on in times of drought. Yes, Martin is a poem I will forever write. A poem that hangs perpetually on the edge of my imagination, always forming, stretching its tentacles of feeling to catch the spirit of desire. To catch the passion resident in the folds of my flesh, the mating partner for the love, which lives within me, for him, who is father of our one child.

He left towards evening that day, after awkwardly trying to say goodbye. I could see the urge in him to be with me alone for a while, to even talk to me in private. I wished I could be in his arms, feel his warm body for a minute, but there was no privacy allowed, even for a hug. Tradition, even if not observed fully, overrode reality, so that we all pretended that Martin had not married me yet, and was therefore not allowed intimacy with me. It was a game well acted and Aunt Mai and her husband stood outside the door like sentinels, bidding him goodbye.

Godbless and I escorted Martin to the bus stop.

"I love this place and the people," he said, showing reluctance to leave. The three of us walking together were targets for people's stares. The women, always hurrying somewhere, emitting the characteristic, warm, wood smoke smell, enquired whether this was the husband they had heard about. "Yes, ma, this is the one," I answered shyly, again and again. They laughed, with a certain plain happiness that indicated approval. Women were more direct in their questions, always suggestive and prying. It concerned them. I was Foibe Seko's only daughter, the one who had beaten some boys by getting education and becoming a big teacher, a salaried woman! And Foibe Seko, without even a husband, without any man!

Martin enjoyed the attention he received from the women who did not talk to him directly. He asked, in a low tone whether the young men also ask the same questions when he was not around. "They don't want to know," I said. Godbless grunted and we laughed.

Martin was reluctant to get into the bus when it came. "Brother, I really would like to take my wife with me. I take her or you let me stay," he complained, laughing, but I knew he meant it.

"O, o, no! Not yet. Some things must take their time, you know," Godbless said, very seriously. He held me by the hand and pulled me to him, as if to prevent me from making any physical contact with Martin, in public. I knew the rules, I had already explained them in detail to Martin. My situation was too delicate to be left to Martin to manage on his own as he had done to me with his people. He knew he had to go.

We stood there on the road until the bus disappeared.

We took our time on our way back, talking excitedly about who said what and how, about Martin's charm and looks and about possibilities for us now.

"He sounds like a good man," Godbless said of Martin. I said, laughing, "Of course! He *is* a good man. Oo, me I love him too much." And Godbless pushed me away jokingly, "Child stuff," he said. "Men think of greater things."

Then Godbless changed the conversation and started talking about himself. "You know sister, I have never really behaved like the first born. You know, first it was not getting education. Then not having a job. It kills me, truly sister."

He looked at me, expecting my acceptance of his predicament, my sympathy.

"It is difficult now. I will never get a job... not even a sweeper in an office."

What was he getting at? I could say something and without knowing, completely upset him, so I decided to wait until he was finished. We were walking slowly, at ease.

"You know, father could have helped. Set me up with some business. Wipe mother's tears by that act."

Godbless would not give up on his father. He wanted so much, so very much to be fathered. But his longing had ceased to affect me by now. I had heard it one time too many .

"What father are you talking about?" I asked

"You know," he said.

I did, but I said, "I don't know him."

He stood still. He looked at me. I could tell it was important by the way he pursed his lips. "I want to tell you something, Doreen." There was urgency in his voice, seriousness. I became expectant. "Yes...?" I urged.

He searched for words. His eyes wore a mellowness that spoke of longing, of sadness. Finally, he said, "When I was little, almost a year after you were born, our father came home to see us. He sat in the sitting room and mother wrapped you in a blanket and brought you to him so he could hold you. You were sleeping. Mother sat there with him and she said to me, 'Godbless, this is your father.' I just shook my head to acknowledge the statement and looked at him. I really do not remember what I saw, but I gazed at him for a long time. I wanted to pull you away and climb into his lap so he could put his arms around me, but I was very afraid of him. All I did instead was stare at him as he touched your face and held your tiny fingers in his and called you 'his mother'. I felt something very sharp in my chest and I went to mother and demanded to be held, climbing on her lap roughly as if she were a tree. Mother laughed, but at least my demand took his attention from you and he looked at me, smiling as if he knew just how I felt. Then he held my hand and asked me to greet him properly before he lifted me off my feet with one hand and put me on his one knee. His one hand was around me and another held you on the other knee. Mother looked so happy. I have never forgotten the shine in her eyes and her face. How different she looked that day! He held us for a long time, talking to me and looking at you alternately. He too looked happy. I could feel it. I did not know it then, could not feel it, but I think he loved mother. I am sure he loved her.

Mother left him with us alone and went to make tea. He looked around the room. He looked at us. He asked me whether I was a good boy and I nodded my head. I never said a word that day. I just nodded my head at everything he asked. Mother brought tea and we all had to leave his knee so he could drink tea. You slept all the time, so mother put you on the bed and the three of us drank tea. They talked guardedly, I thought, like there was a secret between them. I drank my tea quickly and demanded some more. Then I drank quickly again and wanted more. He said, "You will grow into a big man," and mother laughed. After tea, mother said, "Go out Godbless, go and play." I did not want to go away from him, so I refused to leave.

From a small bag he had come with, he took out a parcel and gave it to mother, then he gave me a toy car made from wood. You know, the one that is driven by a stick with a fork on one end. I was so happy sister. I remember that feeling of happiness until today! I see the car vividly. 'I made this just for you,' he told me, smiling. I jumped up and down, showing the car to mother, saying, 'its mine, its mine.' I wanted him to stay with us forever. Not to leave us again. I threw tantrums with mother for her to make him stay. Mother looked at me and he smiled and said, 'I will come again. I will come every day.'

He came again, a long time after that, on an evening when we had already eaten and were ready to go to bed. He did not stay long. He talked with mother and left.

I could not stand his leaving. I cried. I cried so hard. I wanted to go with him, but mother held me back and let him go. I fought mother, forcing her to release me and allow me to go with him. I threw myself on the ground, I bit her hand, but she never even loosened her grip on my hands. I think I continued to cry even in sleep.

He never came again. I used to ask mother why he didn't come, used to beg her to let me go to him, but she never accepted and never explained his absence clearly. I loved him so much. I loved him so dearly, Doreen. I had to find out why it was so, why he could not love us back. I came to know when I was grown enough to ask questions."

Godbless looked up at the treetops and his eyes swam in tears. I kept quiet. I could see the longing come back to his face, that keen desire so tinged with pain. I felt helpless, unable to relieve my brother of the thorn in the tenderness of that memory. What should I tell him?

He finally looked at me and laughed, amid the sadness and the tears, saying, " You never even saw the car! I drove it to pieces in just a short time. I was so proud of it."

We started walking again, in silence. I had nothing to say about our father, I felt no love, no emotional connection. I had no memories of anything he had done to me or mother or even Godbless. I did not remember him to have even held my hand. Like Godbless, I found out he was my father through other people, through my Great Aunt Mai.

"How long will you hold on to that longing, Godbless? You must let it go."

I held his hand. It felt good walking hand in hand like that.

"How do I do that, my sister? Tell me how," he asked.

"I don't know. I wish I did," I said.

I have often remembered that day, with empathy for Godbless. I later came to understand his loss of faith in love, and in loving. What use was it to him if it caused so much pain? I have shared the feeling with him often, the feeling of loving someone who cannot be reached! Today, ten years from that evening, and supposedly wiser, I would still tell him that I don't know the prescription for releasing longing from the heart before it chooses to vacate on its own.

He sighed deeply. "Anyway," he said, as if to hush my mind's inquiry into that well of feeling. He needed to calm his own ripples that memory had stirred. "I don't know why, I just felt this strong urge to tell you something about our father."

"Thank you Godbless," I said.

We walked a distance in silence. He started talking energetically again. "You know, Alfred and Samson must go to secondary school. It won't do for them to be like me," he said.

"Hmm," I agreed, tentatively.

"Mother is aging you know. We boys must have jobs, I mean money, so we can care for her when she is old. It is a lot of responsibility," he said.

"Yes, it is a lot of responsibility," I agreed. "But I will be there to help. I am not going away for good," I said.

"A girl emigrates from the home when she gets married," he said.

"*Ako te*. I can tell you, I have no plans to leave home just because I have a husband. It is my home, why should I leave?"

Ha, haa. I laugh at myself now! I laugh at my naiveté. The assumption that belied Godbless' statement was that I would *have* to *leave* home! *A girl emigrates from the home when she gets married.* Surely, my place would be taken over by his wife! Tradition has it that once a girl is married she acquires other parents, her in-laws, and loses the bonds with her biological parents. It is accepted that her parents will get other daughters through marriage of the sons. So a married woman cannot again sleep at her parent's house. It would be an invasion into the territory of the brothers' wives, trained to excel in verbal warfare by a tradition women sustain but do not own or control.

A married woman will not even stay the night to comfort a parent when one of them dies! No. They should keep their love and sympathy for their in- laws! No amount of feeling should defy this social order! Chaperones accompany her to ensure that the obedience to tradition is maintained.

How many times have I come back to this question, my brother Godbless, chewing and chewing on it like sinewy meat that refuses to give. A woman cannot sleep at her parent's home without the permission of husband and in-laws. "It *cannot* happen!" Aunt Mai had said, laughing at my shock.

This issue clouds my visits home, almost every time, looking at Godbless in the eyes, suspiciously, to see what he is thinking, because I knew I slept there in the room with my mother because of her resolve. "My children will find laughter in my house." I had heard her say over and over to other women in tête à tête, not knowing then the importance of that statement. They had threatened to chase love from Mother's heart, wanting her to be guided by social norms instead. She said, no, love will stay, and so she carried the shock of being unloved by her parents like a boulder on her shoulders. Did she, later in her life, ever wish to be spoilt by her mother? Did she ever wish to stay with her talking late into the night because there was too much for them to share?

Mother went on to be the unusual one, the one who did not get married (or could not after being spoilt?), the strange one who gave her children her own name! When all these things came to mean so much to me, and I noticed that Godbless did not raise the issue of my immigration status, I learned: if a house has a man as head, tradition stays; if there is no man as head, immigration status is not applicable. Were it not for mother, the master architect who gave us all the name Seko, meaning laughter, Godbless' story and mine would have joined here; I who would have to emigrate from home upon marriage, and he, the child come to this world carried on the head! Both of us without a *place*, without a home.

And so I also figured, for a woman to be denied the right of sleeping at her parent's home even in the event of death, she had not only emigrated, she had been *expelled* from the home. It was again, abandonment of the girl, and woman, like a heavy baggage of no or little value.

Home. Why hadn't women redefined the concept, come up with one that applied to them?

That day I said to Godbless, "Maybe you are right, but it need not be like that. I am really not emigrating from the home. My spirit will never leave, can never leave."

I was only refusing to obey a set rule. I had not thought about the matter at all. It was an instinctual response to being expelled from a place I considered rightfully ours, me inclusive. Instinct also told me I could not leave mother, my partner at the hearth wherever I was. The fact that the girl and woman have no *place* reserved for them means that it is not possible for them to leave home. It is the man who should leave, spiritually and physically, to start anew some *place* else, with a girl woman taking the place of mother, to create for him a new hearth and family he will call his own! If people should belong where they are born, it should be women, not men.

"A woman's home is where she is mothering," Great Aunt Mai once told me in reference to my mother.

"And after mothering, Aunt Mai?"

She argued, "Mothering never stops, a woman is either mothering children or the husband." That is why she and Uncle Simbo had given mother a place, a piece of earth with soil and stones and trees for her to mother her children and make a home. She knew and accepted both sides of the equation, just like she took a pregnant young woman expelled from home, nurtured her physically and psychologically, then claimed her as child in order to avert danger to her life!

Sometimes I tried to add meaning into Aunt Mai's statement by saying that mothering could mean a woman's biology, so that by extension, a woman's home is in her own biology. If that is all there is for her, then own it, make it a power base that can never be claimed or given to others! Next time I will ask Aunt Mai, " Are women owned by themselves in their biologies?"

That day Godbless talked, perhaps spurred by Martin's visit. He talked of starting to construct his house. He wanted a small but good house. He solicited my opinion about how it should be and we talked with enthusiasm about it. The house was already built really, it already had shape and character in his mind. He talked, briefly about the kind of girl who would live in that house with him. He knew her!

"My wife must respect me, you know. So it is important that a man has a house, a good one, before he marries," he said.

I looked at him. 'My house, my wife, a man must have money.' He was already a man. It occurred to me then that his desire to be a separate entity, to identify with the father, to belong to the world of men, distinctly apart from the mother, was a thing beyond the decision of the conscious mind. It was the logical route of the thread in the matrix of maleness.

We had walked for a while and he took my hand again. There was magic in that declaration from Godbless, that open statement of friendship shown in him holding my hand in a gesture other than a handshake. It was the first time it had ever happened. It seemed like a parting gift. That was the closest I ever have been with him, in that silence, holding hands and feeling, without naming it, the binding love between siblings whose lives are at a crossroads. A woman passed us and then a man. Both greeted us warmly and both turned to look again. We did not unlock our hands. Somehow, we had found in ourselves, without thinking, the rebellion against what was acceptable, which is necessary for individual freedom. We walked in silence. We could feel the last warmth of early night wrapping our spirits in protective magnanimity.

We stayed up late after dinner and talked about plans to open a small shop at the house. I felt that mother and son had already discussed it. It would not be too big, she said, it would carry only a few items. Everything had been planned. Mother was confident that the shop would be a source of income for Godbless. She flowered in authority as she talked of her children's future. "Doreen, you will have to see how these things will go," she said, pleading in her subtle way, for help. "I have no energy now to work too hard and this child has to have something," she added to emphasize the necessity for my support.

I promised as much support as I could commit with my teacher's salary. I knew, at the back of my mind, that I was just trying to prove that I would not leave home. I also knew that they depended on me.

When the issue of marriage for Godbless came up again, steered in by mother's expert ways, I waited for the girl's name to be announced. Godbless allowed mother to talk about it for a long time.

"Who is she?" I asked.

Godbless kept quiet. Mother, trying not to spoil the mood, said, "Do not worry, Doreen. It is enough that he has decided to marry. It is quite enough. A girl will be found."

Godbless sat back and listened to his mother plan his future. He had it all planned, but he indulged his mother by letting her feel she was guiding him, or perhaps they had already discussed the matter too? Mother concluded by saying that it was good Martin came, that now there is a face to her daughter's husband.

After she had tucked herself into bed, she said to me in the dark, "Go with God and stay with God."

"Thank you, ma," I said.

I left in the morning to join Martin in town, ready for our journey to Dar es Salaam.

PART THREE

Ashes and Embers

*The evolutionary impulse towards wholeness calls us
to undertake an earth walk, on a planet where limitation
and opposition seem to rule, to live (life) fully in all its
beautiful and terrifying complexity, in a place
where wholeness seems not possible...*

Joseph Jastrab
Sacred Manhood, Sacred Earth, 1994

CHAPTER 14

Marriage is like walking in the rain, in the cold, wet season, without an umbrella. You get soaked through to the skin before you know what's happened. You get possessed by the rain, by the wet clothes which cling to your body, marking its curves out like a claimed territory. Then, you are imprisoned in that state, that of the rain falling on you and the clothes possessing your body like a territory.

The choices are hard. You cannot choose between standing still or taking off your clothes, because there would be no difference at all, standing put in one place in the rain; or walking with your clothes off. That state tends to invite other threats, disease, loss of reason. The choice open to you, then, is one; walking on, clothes and all. This way, you at least, meet the rain head on, meet it and leave some of it behind as you walk, as you make the inevitable movement forward.

That is why I cannot concretely describe what came between Martin and me. That is why I am still walking on.

At a time I do not remember, we became orphans of our senses, they being at once the bridge that connected us, and the chasm that estranged us. Everything took us by surprise. There was the stream of relations who wanted Martin to replace their fathers, mothers, husbands and wives and provide for their lives. There was the issue of keeping house; that was not a big problem because there was always help, first the sister and the house girl, and after the sister left the house girl proved quite efficient. There was the issue of having a child. That one was quite welcome; after all, we had planned for four of them. Martin's job, had to be respected, he had to be supported in every possible way because it meant money and another house. The one we were living in was going to be too small when the children came. We needed a car. That was a matter of urgency because after getting married, Martin felt himself rise a notch in the social ladder. It would be good indeed to have a car, even a second hand one. I tried to be a good wife and a teacher too.

With all the planning and anxiety to define our place in society, marriage still made us one entity, so that we thought as one, continued to plan our life as one, easily adapting to surprises. We were sure of things too - the food we wanted to eat, the places we wanted to go, the clothes we loved on each other's bodies, our favorite friends. The sex and the freedom to seek it from each other; the intimacy which gave us access to each other's bodies, like a door opening into a familiar room.

"That bud you love is craving to flower," I would croon, seductively.

"Oh, God, let me see," he would say, gently parting my legs as if something extremely fragile nestled there.

I could just turn in sleep, and Martin would know whether I was awake or still asleep. Early in the morning, before sleep leaves the body, Martin would raise the wake up alarm, "Dori, please, wake up the boneless, lazy guy there," underlining the 'there' in a slow, sleepy croak.

"Hmm," I would agree, but would not move.

"Dori, the guy needs to know what's up," he would urge, with a little more energy, with a voice suddenly devoid of sleep, pleading a bit. He would move closer, his hand finding my body under the covers, traveling along the well -known routes to passion.

Martin knew so many jokes. So many ugly and dirty but funny jokes: "I hear you have a friend with a terrible habit. He vomits every time he eats."

"Who? Me? Never!"

"Oh, yes. I am told you love him for that!"

There was so much laughter between us. That was the time we would laugh at everything that sounded funny in our ears.

That was also the time I became pregnant and joy came into our house bringing with it gifts of love and concern for each other the whole period of nine months. Martin would cook or walk the restaurants to buy me some food I craved. He became a knot of concern if I fell sick with malaria. He was concerned about my teaching job that made me stand up the whole day. It is simply not good for any woman, he would complain, almost everyday, especially after the sixth month of pregnancy. He made me take my leave two months before time so he would be sure that I was not overworking myself or the pupils were not irritating me too much.

He came home on time when I was home, beaming and talking of the challenges of his job as if they were not challenges at all. I prepared his food myself, a fact he loved. I served him, I sat with him as he ate and he insisted that we take a rest together. And often, we made love tenderly, tenderly, because, he said, the baby must not feel that his father was deliberately being cantankerous. "I am told that these little creatures can know everything, you see. One must respect them even before they arrive," he would say.

"Choose a name for him," he would tell me and continue immediately, hurriedly, without giving me the chance. "My choice is Freedom. I would like him to break free from the social traps we lay for ourselves. No man should find himself in my father's shoes. No man should."

"Its okay. He is going to be okay. Everybody is given a load he or she can carry. God is that kind," I would tell him, softly massaging his forehead, wanting to chase away the shadow of his father from our bed.

"Should I choose a name? My choice is Milika, she will be blessed," I said.

Freedom and Milika. These remained the most favored names out of the many we chose during the nine months. And Milika came first.

His sister, Rebeka, came to help when the baby was born. She knew everything that needed to be done for me and with the baby. Milika had Martin's eyes and a face that promised to have pronounced cheekbones. It made him ecstatic. "You know, it helps for a man to be reassured," he said. He loved her and would call for her the moment he came through the door. Either the baby sitter or me would say that she was sleeping or is being bathed. Joy stayed in our house longer, filling our hearts with gratitude for having a child. We lavished Milika with attention until the sister-in-law was quite concerned, saying that children should never be loved like that, it spoils them.

Rebeka decided to focus on me. "Women are the pillars of the home. Women raise children and men," she said to me one day after observing my relationship with Martin and concluding that we were behaving like children!

"Women have the company of women and men have the company of men, I should know that," she said to me, in the middle of conversation with Martin about inviting some of his friends for dinner to mark his birthday.

Martin and I stopped the conversation. He looked at me in the eyes and said, "I will be right back," and stood up to go.

"Where are you going?" I asked.

"I am just going out a bit," he said.

He knew I needed him, but his sister's statement had already pushed us into the circle of a bigger force that had caught us by surprise. So, he left me with his sister, who did her best to amuse me.

"Men live in the world of men and come in the world of women and the home to sleep and make children," my sister-in-law said, with mirth. She had been married before and no doubt was speaking from experience. She was happy, she proclaimed, laughing. She had such capacity to laugh at life! In a way, I envied her capacity and skills. I supposed that to understand and accept that layer of reality and find happiness in it made life infinitely easier.

"*Wifi*, why do you love men like that?" she asked, her face full of genuine concern. What was I to say? I kept quiet and she continued, "Why should you need a man all the time?"

I could sense resentment in her voice, a bit of anger too. I could not be sure whether this was for the benefit of her brother or me. I chose to think it was for me.

"Isn't other women's company good enough for you?"

She was the adult woman teaching me, a young woman, the

basic rules of survival, I concluded. It must have been exasperating for her, because she expected me to know better. My sister-in-law loved the company of women, she thought men were boring creatures, wrapped in the problems of their plain life. These are the problems that made them sulky. I should not hang on a man all the time when all he does is complain and nag!

I got her point. I absorbed that lesson. She stayed with me for two months before she went back to her family.

I could not tell precisely when the emptiness settled in. It could have started slowly, with the sister-in-law's expert teachings for her brother and me. But it slipped into our life, casually, like a vagabond who comes to shelter and stays, blending into the family, acquiring character that marked us out individually, being an inseparable part of us.

Later, after Martin was gone from all of us, I forgave the sister-in-law and imagined that the emptiness in our life was brought in by our own urge for a male child. Coming to us in bed, almost taking the part of foreplay. Martin pleading; "*Mpenzi*, lets make a boy child, *please*," so tender that pledge, so involving the sex, so wholesome. I forgot the determinate one was he. I tried, without knowing how, having nothing to hold on to, nothing to use to pry the male seed from him. I tried. Freedom, where are you? My soul called.

When seduction did not work, when impatience was the more obvious, the urge went out of bed into the sitting room where it found relatives and friends.

"Now after Milika, a boy. What are you waiting for? These days you get two or three children when you are young so that they grow up with you."

Milika walked when she was a year and half. She was slow, her father had already started to worry. When she finally made her steps, Martin changed the furniture, removed some things from the sitting room so that she could find space enough to practice her new skill. At two she was already saying words, '*baba taka*; *baba joo*.' Then they became real friends, talking away as I prepared their food, washed their clothing, made their beds; assured their comfort.

They started going out together for walks or for a drive. All she needed to say was; "*Baba, tende*," and off they would go.

Slowly, the attention was moving away from each other to Milika.

"*Mama, bebe*." She would demand that I carry her and play with her just when Martin had come home. She would cry until I did just what she wanted. I would have to go out if that is what she wanted. Other times, she would say, "*Baba kula*," and demand that her father feeds her. We did not know it, but we had started converging on Milika, Martin and I, because we were not talking to each other so much any more. Each of us started competing for her attention and love. We needed it, and went for it like thirsty people craving for water. We spoilt her in the process, because Milika, in her God given natural instinct, recognised our thirst and our need and frolicked in it. She knew how to make us want her laughter. She knew when we craved her attention. She knew how we would feel if she did not eat, or sleep in the afternoon or refuse to take a bath. We danced on the rope she stretched out for us, consciously unaware, but guided by a rich subconscious, older than her and by far, wiser. We enjoyed the game for the respite it afforded us. Sometimes the little daemon inside her would rise and Milika would cry endlessly for something minor she was forbidden to have or do. She would not be comforted. No temptations of presents of any kind would appease her. It hurt us, it worried me and angered Martin who was always able to escape and go away somewhere to drink. But like all parents, after her anger was spent, we forgave her mischief. We showered her with gifts of all kinds, Ah, Milika was the star in our life, she became our love and she gave herself in that way, unreservedly.

Why couldn't Martin be happy with her?

The discussion about being pregnant was no longer a topic in our bedroom, but its presence, mute and ominous, followed us even as we breathed silently in our sleep. It started working on both of us until it broke us in like a new pair of shoes that pinch. Our initial dreams became cobwebs to be wiped away. We could no longer look at our wanting a child from afar, saying that a girl child was a child like any other, just as good as any boy child. We started talking like our friends, like my in- laws, that a boy child would really bless our marriage. I started believing that it would make Martin so happy, that it would be good for Milika. A brother would pull the attention from her to him. She too needed another child in the family to love. That subtle pressure kneaded us to softness of mind so that Martin and I entered into the core of that want willingly, humbly, carrying our need like a prayer

We went to the doctor. He said that both of us were okay, we would have children. I was so happy, so hopeful. The child would choose its time, I thought and relaxed into the hope. But in no time, Martin was asking,

"But why can't you get pregnant, Doreen? What is wrong with you?"

The only tangible way to take, the one we both knew, was my

body, the most effective bridge to Martin other than speech. But both of us had to walk that bridge into each other, where a mystical touch between human seeds would take form and breath and spirit. Why was blame meted out to me alone?

I refused to take the blame. I refused to be a scapegoat. My body felt fecund, warm, and secretive. I told him so and I tried to discuss the situation in a different way, reminding him of what the doctor had told us. He was silent.

"What are you suggesting, Doreen? You think I am the one who is not fecund and warm? Is that what you think?"

"Martin, love of my life, how can I suggest that you are not warm? What reason do I have to say that you are not fecund? May be we are just too anxious?"

"Ha! Can you not see? It runs in the family. It is just too bad for you, Doreen. Sorry, you do not deserve this," he said, sadly, resignedly.

"Martin, look at me. Look at me," I was almost shouting, almost crying. I took his face like a baby's in both my hands, made him look into my eyes and promised, "Freedom will be born to you. You will *get* him."

A long, long time ago when human beings were confused about what to do with such a vast, vast world, the wise ones said that we, human beings, carry miracles in our hands. The wise ones said that we are short sighted to know it ourselves. It is all here in our hands! That is how change which shapes the world is realised. This piece of wisdom came to mind, like a flash of light, when I allowed Joseph a place in my heart.

That day, all I felt was the sadness brought up by Martin's fear of being like his father, of ending up like his father had ended up.

My eyes welled with tears as I hugged him, trying to tell him that it would not happen to him.

"I hate being pitied," is what he said, pulling himself away from my embrace and leaving the room. It was night. I heard him start the car and leave.

And so withdrawal started like a thin crack on the wall of our life. I watched it grow and widen. I was helpless, unable to mend something that I did not determine alone. He started coming late, armed with excuses - the workload in the office; the friends with a problem that only he could solve; the tiredness, first generally, then in bed; and finally, outright indifference. Passion, that was like a tonic in our life, withered. It felt like an ugly, shrinking part of my body. The absence of it singed like fire on the skin.

The mood in the house changed, naturally. It became downcast and depressing. The house was always dark somehow, as though the windows were no longer adequate to bring in enough sunlight and air.

The house girl tried to be friendly to me, but I was like a rash. I made her, the only adult around me, itch. Milika was so full of exuberance she did not see the downcast mood. The neighborhood had many children the same age and older than her. She was the pet. All girls wanted to play with her, so immediately after school, when I heard, "Teacher...," from a young voice, I knew they were asking me if Milika could go with them to play.

"Milika, your friends are asking for you," I would shout to her and she would come out of her room where she had been playing by herself almost the whole day, run past me like an arrow and shoot out without even seeing me. It was a rule that she plays inside the house or within the compound when we were at work. But when I came home, I did not spend time with her. I allowed her to go out to play even before we spent time together. There were days we did not see each other till evening at table during dinner. The house girl knew her life better than me.

I feel so guilty every time I remember this period of our life and realize how easily I was also abandoning her!

The house girl was committed to the mission of empathizing with me. Although she never spoke a word, she knew everything that was happening between Martin and me. I never knew how much they talked with my sister-in-law, but she always seemed the sympathetic one. And in this, she never gave up. She was more than obliging in this, preparing all kinds of food for me all the time, bringing it into the bedroom when I was too depressed to wake up. I ate, all the time. She did not know about depression, she just figured that I liked her food, she thought I was being friendly. I ate everything, including the stuff I prepared myself, and that which I bought when I went out of the house. It was as though I needed to smother the churning in the body with the pile of food. I ballooned everywhere, my stomach swelled, my breasts, ankles, hands fattened. My whole body sagged, overrun by too much weight and the gravity of abandonment. I developed a hatred for mirrors!

But no amount of food or the house girl's sympathy would assuage the sexual urge that boiled inside me like rumbling, burning lava, unable to find a weak spot through which to erupt.

One day, I looked at myself in the mirror, by accident really, because I didn't mean to, and I saw something too obese to be me! What had I done to myself?! I heard a thin voice inside me say, 'let the heartache lie, Doreen. Arrest the passion.' I had just taken a bath but I slumped on the bed without drying myself and thought;

how do I do it? How do I stop killing myself? And as though on
cue, I stumbled on a decision:
When he is away, feel nothing
When you see him, feel nothing
When you hear his voice, feel nothing
When he is near you, feel nothing
When you feel nothing, you are free.

CHAPTER 15

Dear Friend Doreen, I am inviting you to my wedding...

Zima was getting married. That was okay, but the thing that shook me up was that he was marrying because it was getting late for him: "I need a wife and children," he said.

The girl he was marrying was not educated, but was very nice, he said. Kind, understanding, patient, and had all the things he could not get from me because I 'was too stubborn, too selfish and self centered.' Yet, he said, he very often thinks of me, what I made him feel. He has not been able to fall in love again, he said. "I feel you like a sixth finger on my hand, a finger that was amputated. My hand is complete with the five fingers, but the stamp of the sixth finger haunts me always."

Is this wrong? he asked.

Is it wrong for a man to marry a woman because she is kind, patient and understanding while he harbors desire and love for another?

Doesn't Martin's infidelity ask me the same question? Is it wrong for a man to go searching for a desired male child in a woman other than his wife even when the wife loves him like life itself?

I sent Zima a very expensive wedding card.

I trained myself to think of things outside my personal life. I focused on the day to day struggles. The Headmaster had to be made happy. That way, a teacher wards off trouble. It was, however, not hard for me because I loved teaching and spending time on extra curricular activities. I excelled in that; I got a lot of activities going for the school income generation projects. *River Pebbles Club* had taught me that maintaining friendship with colleagues at work was as important and delicate as keeping lovers, so I trod carefully. I spent time with fellow women teachers, inviting them to my house, going window shopping together, going to the tailors and to the gold smith.

As for Martin, (who by now was a life outside my personal one), I tried to please his friends so that he was not thought to be dominated by his wife, so that I could deserve him. The silent struggles slowly mutated me into a woman known as Mrs. Patrick, a product that resembled Doreen Seko, while Doreen Seko herself went under ground.

And did I understand how Mrs Patrick was to live?

I know that I let myself be shaped by what people wanted me to be. I ceased to fight so that I could be Mrs. Doreen Patrick. As Aunt Mai would say, 'a woman should sit, sit until the buttocks touch the grass.' Bend the iron while it is hot! That is what my sister-in-law was trying to do. It took me so long to arrive at that lesson, so long to understand it.

That is also how, rather late in life, and no longer as malleable, marriage took its proper place and became my school. I lived on campus and had good teachers in the persons of sisters-in-laws, neighbors and friends, themselves first class graduates. I learned that gossip is survival for women. It is a vent for excessive creative capacity born out of long periods of lonely imaginings of where their husbands, once their lovers, could be, what they could be doing. The longer the hours of absence, the sharper the creativity. The best subject for gossip being relations between women and men, love affairs failed as well as successful, abandonment, poverty and wealth. I learned that in gossip women found laughter, satiation, a catharsis that was a mirage to be sought, perpetually.

Lessons from the past follow me like a smitten admirer who must ensure that he is noticed and acknowledged. I came to admit that the demise of the River Pebbles Club at Sokoni Juu was not really caused by gossip. We made teaching aids, yes, but gossip was what kept bringing the women together. It made the women a 'group' when they shared what each brought to the sessions; their secret lives and those of husbands and friends; their opinions about others. What really caused the break up was that I did not participate in sharing. I became a spectator, an observer in a club that allowed only members. The crime: treason. The punishment: abandonment.

Sometimes, after I had come home from school, the neighbors came to visit and to talk. We sat together talking and always, inevitably, after talking about children and food, the subject moved to men. I was the youngest and least experienced in the group and so deserved to be warned, just in case I was naïve, never to be friends with men even if they were colleagues. "They are shrewd, they are smart and can easily fool a woman with cheap presents or money, especially when a woman is young and beautiful and ignorant of the ways of the town." So I should know that men had no right to talk and confide in me, no right to laugh and find happiness together with me, no right at all to come close. I should avoid them. I should *not* trust them.

I listened and laughed with them, because all this was said amid much laughter and camaraderie spiced by real life examples of young women who had fallen victim to the wiles of men. Mostly, we enjoyed what happened to the women or speculated on what was going to happen. "She was such a fool to do it so openly. The husband threw her out like a dog, believe me, like a dog!" Or, "That one, her day is coming. The man she is with isn't anything compared to the husband, and the way the lover dresses the woman! The husband can't say a word. She beats him like a child!" This would be accompanied by laughter and further elaboration.

The daemon in me stirred and laughed. Do you fit the women's mode? it asked.

Do I?

At Sokoni Juu, a group of teachers, mobilized by me met to do things that enhanced their profession, the making of teaching aids. Gossip was an expression of their other layer, that is, what they were other than teachers. When I broke the rules, I was rightly punished. These neighbor women, friendly married women, working as housewives, came to see another married woman, a housewife and a teacher. They quite rightly wanted to orient me in what it takes to be a housewife, a good one, so that I could survive as one. They gave me tips on how to balance the needs of being both a teacher and a woman who was settling into housewifery.

Do women choose to fit the mode or do they find themselves in it?

The daemon laughed. *Know yourself,* it whispered.

A woman must have several lives indeed, just to exist!

Then I understood why mothers repeat those same things to

their girl children. Why structures were designed to ensure systematic re-creation of the whole personality of the girl, like creating masks for a life masquerade. This was meant to minimize the harm! Shape her when she is malleable to fit the conditions of the web.

What goes on in the soul inside the mask?

What does this masquerade turn a girl and woman into?

Oh, mother, what steel you had! What an incredible will! And you so young, when you had to make choices. What a sharp sense of self!

My teachers on the subject of marriage told me that decisions no longer belonged to me to make. Why should I make decisions when I had a man to make them for me? That is why they are men, to make decisions, and that is why they are the head of the house? Weren't Martin's decisions satisfactory to me? Women who make decisions want to domineer, always wanting to be heard and to boss the man around. A very unnatural thing indeed! A woman loved her husband and showed it by trusting in what he did, what he said, what he made of himself. A good woman hid her distrust and doubts in her heart, fighting them like a good soldier fights to defend a cause laid out by the leader...

We talked for hours, sometimes serious, sometimes joking, laughing at the realities of a woman's existence. We ate and drank whatever was available. When it was time to cook the evening meals, they would leave, inviting me to visit them too and assuring me of their friendship.

"Remember I am a working woman, I have very little time," I defended myself.

"My dear, ah, for me, my husband is my pension," the neighbor said. "I have no worries," she concluded. Both of us laughed.

And so it went on like that.

Good morning Mrs. Patrick

Good morning children

Hello Mrs. Patrick

Hello Bwana Abdala

How is Martin

Martin is fine. And how is Mrs. Abdala

I tried.

I draw lessons from the spider's web, woven from the very juices of its stomach to attract others to the web, and kill them - for itself! How do women fit in the social web, in the norms and traditions perpetuated and maintained to keep order, strengthen identity and maintain peace? In this web, she must learn to hide exuberance from her inner feelings because the expression of it may be unacceptable; she must be able to have children; she must have a male child; must be a proper Mrs someone; she should *never* have a child before marriage; she must bear the right number of sons, and on and on...

Three reactions from which to choose a way for my salvation: Great Aunt Mai: adapt and master the skills of survival. Mother: rebel and have enough steel in yourself to survive. Martin's mother: corrode your inside with bitterness and then use it as poison.

"A woman is a social orphan indeed, just by being," said Great Aunt Mai. She had lived within the social web and learned her lessons.

The issue of the male child had become a wall between Martin and I. When I tried again to make us talk, he assured me that things were all right. He had not changed. He was quite happy with me.

He loved me. He advised me to settle down and be happily married. Wasn't I happy with him as husband? What was he not doing?

The struggle to want to understand the other side of love which was really not hate seemed like a weight on my soul. It conditioned my thinking, the understanding of myself as a woman and wife, the understanding of Martin as a man and my husband, my thinking about marriage and social expectations. I tried to confide in a male teacher who seemed wise to me by the things he did and the advice he often gave to others.

He laughed at my concern and said, "To be honest, Martin is right. There is nothing wrong. He loves you. You know, when a man is married, everything becomes available easily: respect, food, sex, clean clothes and a well-kept house. Even our relatives, mother, sisters and even cousins are cared for without the man lifting a finger. Finally the situation settles into a permanence that is normal, predictable and good. That is the state every man wants in marriage.

Now, about the issue of you not getting a male child, you see, women and men do not have the same choices. A man can say; I want my marriage, I love my woman, so I will try to strike my luck elsewhere. In that, a man has a choice to bring home the child born outside marriage, after a certain time. Or, he could take the other woman as a second wife. Women cannot do that, because men do not want them to do that. So, I still think Martin is right. He has chosen his marriage. He has chosen you as *the* wife."

Yes, but I found it colorless. Of course, I was not a man. That was a life I was supposed to maintain for Martin. I was the *creator* of the life and not the recipient. Where then was *my* life? Settle down and be happily married, is what Martin had said. So there, the answer to my question was quite clear. My life was called *normal life*. I was to live it, accept it and wear it like my own skin!

I tried, resentment notwithstanding.

I walked on in the rain, soaked to the bone. What was I to do? My marriage gave in to the routine of waking and doing the daily ministrations and sleeping and when Martin was up to it, making love which was familiar, without newness. It seemed like mutiny to demand freshness in sex. When I decided to enjoy sex because the body was pulsing from the accumulation of its own sap, because it had become a taut knot wanting release, the heat inside simmering for a vent, it was a problem! Who was I thinking of as I made love? Why was I so sexy? When I did not enjoy it, because it was expected and demanded like a plate of rice with meat, taken as a right, when my body would be completely removed from the act, then it would be; who else is making you satisfied?

Fascination for each other evaporated into this normality. And the daemon inside me tired, because life unfolded, daily, under an opaque light, without energy for renewal and creation. Color went away from marriage and left a reality too tedious and dreary; it doused the spirit.

Sometimes in the course of my teaching day, standing in front of the pupils, a question would steal into my mind: Could this normality have made me barren?

I had started thinking that perhaps *I* was barren, until Joseph came into my life and said, simply, "Do not carry another person's load. It is better to try to sympathize and understand. Guilt and insecurity do not nurture love, understanding does." He made me see the way with just those few words.

Almost every evening, Martin went out, leaving me with Milika who became my companion, my confidante, friend and child at the same time. Thinking back, I wonder if I did not hurt her by my rancor, when I went on and on about the unfairness of things. I feel guilty, thinking back to that recent past, when I realized that Milika did not deserve to be biased against her father. I could see that his absence became like an entity both of us could touch, making it more confusing for her who did not know what was happening.

The shower of attention Martin poured on Milika waned with time.

"Mama, where does father go these days? He is never here with us as when I was little," she would say.

"Your father is a busy man, Milika. He has to work hard in order to bring you more toys and good clothes."

"I don't need any more toys and clothes," she would say, sulking, stamping her feet in frustration. She had already turned seven years, was in standard one and starting to question and analyze things.

Milika's unfed gullibility for attention turned to open rebellion. The older she grew the more we quarreled. Her attention went to her father, who she missed because she saw him rarely. Baba was good, baba was not angry with her, did not scold her, and was not mean. Mama became the unfriendly parent she could afford to fight. Martin was sure that another child would solve the problem of Milika's stubbornness. "She needs another child to take her attention. She needs to see our attention going to another child," he said, desperately. I could see the helplessness he felt with the situation. He loved this child, but the love for this one did not remove desire for the other. I could see it.

One day, crazed by desperation, I took the bus and went home.

It was not clear in my mind what I was going for, what miracle I expected to achieve. The journey allowed me thinking time and on the way, I realized that I was the little girl running home to mother to cry, to appeal for her protection and support.

They were all surprised to see me. Things had changed, the mood in the home had brightened up, perhaps because the shop was up and going and because finally Godbless had got himself a fiancé, a teacher from the neighboring village school. "With money sister, a man is a man," he said, confidently. He emphasized that fact as if to tell me that he too could achieve learning and success through a different route. But I had my own problems this time. It was me who was quiet and withdrawn, one who talked less.

Mother saw this, but remained silent and allowed me time. Mother's silence spoke volumes. I could see she felt my predicament, she even knew it already. But I felt, somehow, we would not be able to deal with this together. My mother took time to open up and talk, as if her words came from too far away, deep down in herself. So I chose Aunt Mai, the more practical one, more down to earth Mai who did not step on a hurt to feel the harshness of its thorn before she could know how to deal with it. Usually, Aunt Mai went around a hurt, advising you not to step on it too long, if you must.

I took her some sugar and rice and money. I gave Uncle Simbo some money too. And I sat with Aunt Mai alone, in the out kitchen, drinking tea. "Okay, talk. Just talk, women affairs carry no shame when said to another woman," she said. She knew I had a problem! She did not immediately drink her tea, she said, "Let mine cool a bit." And when I did not know how or where to start, she jolted me into soberness by saying, "Girl child, I have work to do!"

I opened my heart to her

Aunt Mai was silent for a long time. She drank her tea and finished and asked me if I wanted more. I took another cup of tea.

She let me drink and finish before she said; "*Women of the road* have never broken a woman's marriage. Not if there is no other problem. Should the man love the woman, then he will take or treat her as a wife. He will sleep there in her house without hiding from anyone, even you. But not even that will break a woman's marriage. Always, it is a woman who *keeps* a marriage, if there is no problem."

Aunt Mai looked at the hearthstones as she said this. I listened to her, a bit surprised at what she had said, but I listened. I did not interrupt her. "If your husband says he loves you, then he loves you."

"The other thing, that one is difficult. *Yee le*! Children go into marriage as into a wilderness," she lamented. She was finding it hard to talk, looking at me with pity in her eyes.

What was it, Aunt Mai? My mind screamed in a silent panic.

"Take another cup of tea," she urged me.

"No, Aunt Mai. I am full," I said.

Finally she said, "A woman will know where the problem is when a child does not come. A woman will know. She will know because she has knowledge of her man, and she has knowledge of her body. The spirit which gives people children, and which lives in all of us, will be mute and cold if a woman is barren. And so a woman will know where the problem is. A woman must be true to this spirit. So, if she is barren, and she has accepted it, she will go out and look for a woman to give her marriage children. She will tell her man when she has found the woman to give them children. A man will have children with the woman, and they will be the children of both women. The children will call both women, 'mother'. Yes, that is how it was done.

Now, if a woman is not barren, if the spirit that gives children does not feel like cold ash in her body, it will still be her who looks for a child, *not* a man. Never. It is the woman who looks around her, *carefully*. She looks around her man, and being guided by the spirit that gives a woman the ability to keep life inside her until it is a person, she chooses the man who will give her children. Nobody should breath this out, not you and not the man, no matter what happens, not even before death will the matter ever come up. That is what we used to do, and all families had children. Look around you," she said again.

The conversation itself had not lasted more than half an hour. It was the kind of subject that does not drag on and on because it doesn't need elaboration or hyperbole. Aunt Mai had no root or grass potions for me, no prescriptions of what I had to do to myself or to Martin, just woman wisdom for my soul.

"Sit down until your buttocks touch the grass and think. Look around you. Now, go to your husband."

That is how she said goodbye.

I returned to Dar es Salaam in total stupor, emptied of any ability to think.

CHAPTER 16

I left with Milika in the morning to go to school and brought her back at mid morning until she was able to make the journey herself. She grew independent from us as her world of school and friends started taking shape. I could see her independence taking root in her personality, in the way she did her school work, the way she chose her friends and what to do with them and when, in the foods she liked and didn't like. No one could make her do things against her will.

Milika ran off with friends all the time, feeling, without knowing concretely, the slow bleeding of happiness out of the home. As an only child, she had learned that her wishes were rights, so she assumed that she could do anything she wanted, without any restraint from us. Milika claimed things, she did not ask. When she had to, she learned to ask without asking. "Mama, I am going to study with my friend, Jesica."

"You are supposed to ask if it is possible, if you can go now, if there is something I need you to do," I would say.

"Can I go now?" she would say, ready to leave, ignoring the possibility that I might refuse her. Sometimes I refused her wishes, but it meant that I had to be with her, to talk to her, help her with homework, engage her in conversation. Sometimes she hated it, sometimes it would turn out well, after some initial sulking.

I started going out, visiting friends and relatives. I had made friends easily in church, in weddings and other social gatherings. I did a lot of voluntary work that took me away from home. Every relative, close and distant who was getting married had me as a dependable helper. I was always ready to offer help. I found happiness in crowds in which Mrs Patrick, the sociable, selfless, friendly and helpful woman was loved and sought after. I enjoyed that reputation, and always did more in order to maintain it and keep the other lonely self away from my consciousness.

I can afford to shake my head and smile now, looking back at the struggle it took to rise from the fine dust of self pity. *When you feel nothing, you are free.* Yes, but that was the hardest of all, feeling nothing. I think after failing to feel nothing, I devised ways that alienated me from myself. I became what is called selfless. I could forget to comb my hair because I was too involved in a friend's birthday party, having to worry more about the food, the plates and decorations than the friend herself. So I would be covered in sweat, tired and dirty when the guests arrived. Then I would refuse to sit down and join the guests because the work of serving food and drinks needed supervision!

Milika was quite satisfied with being left in the care of the house girl because she could do anything she wanted. The house girl could not manage her tantrums and could therefore not forbid her anything. Milika had also acquired many friends, being a crowd puller herself, so the house was always full and busy when the parents were out. Martin would not hear of bringing one of his stepmother's children to give Milika company, so she brought her own friends over for dinner or to sleep over. The house girl, again, was more than willing to indulge them with food. Martin traveled out of town quite regularly. Sometimes he took his girlfriend on those official trips. She was by now not a secret to me anymore. I lived with that knowledge like a secret disease that was taboo to talk about. The only comfort was that she was not yet pregnant.

I excused my uncontrollable eating and drinking to Martin who started being alarmed at my size. "Life is short," I told him. "Every minute of it should be captured and enjoyed." He never argued with me. He looked at my overflowing flesh and kept silent.

In the eyes of some friends, I had indeed found satisfaction in life. I ate and got fat because I could afford to buy the food and drink, which meant I had money. If I had money, life was good! I accepted their reasoning.

How strange, the unfolding of life, I came to realize. Love, after all, has two journeys; both of which are lived in the body, the body I was slowly, gradually extinguishing. The first, the journey into love, starts with the first sparks of desire, at the identification of the other. Then follows the wanting and longing, the smoldering of passion towards coupling. The magic, the crystallizing of body currents into that one intimidating sensation...ends the first journey.

The second journey is the return into self and the meeting with truths. This is the journey of knowledge, where twin landmarks are encountered side by side; hope and despair; expectation and defeat.

'And what are your truths, Doreen?' the daemon asked, raising its head.

That I changed, after loving Martin. After the act of sex with him, I would never be the same again, body and mind. He took something from me, but also left something of him with me, something like a feeling which permeated the texture of my flesh so that it continues to linger on around the heart like the after taste of food.

'*When you feel nothing, you are free,*' it teased.

I have come to greatly appreciate my mother's silence over her inner life, over love and all that came in the same package. It is a lonely road down there. Now, my question to her would be; "How did you keep the laughter, mother, in spite of everything that happened?"

The lessons that informed her life were coming home to roost. She had taught me without saying a word that a woman carries a whole world in her soul. That the struggle with this burden conditions her life, shapes it. Sometimes, when life's trials become too heavy, her spirit escapes the vitality in the glow of her face, taking refuge in the dark corners of her used flesh where she lets it sit, like disease, before the symptoms rise and bed in her eyes. That is how you can tell whether a woman is unhappy or sad, when the tiredness filters through the eyes like muted light through a screen.

Didn't I see this everyday in myself? Hadn't I already pushed my spirit to the dark corner, where it sat like a poor orphan? I have laid down arms in the struggle! Looking at my mother's life as it passed before my eyes, I again recognized how she had refused to let the apathy home in her flesh like a disease. Mother had fought life with a keen love for life. *Fight life with life! Don't let them refuse you now!* I could hear her voice as if she was standing right beside me in that minute.

Oh, mother, how could Godbless ever think I could leave home?

That was the day I almost missed my class for the first time, and the fellow teacher was worried that I could be sick. I found the class riotous and happy, that for once they were left on their own. I entered the class in a good mood and order was restored immediately.

"*Shikamoo Mwalimu,*" they chorused amidst noisy pulling and pushing of chairs.

"*Marhaba,*" I said.

The sun shone, a cool wind found unrestrained entry through open gaps called windows. I could not start teaching a topic, so I gave the pupils some homework. I sat at my desk and felt elation at the resolution that had come to me that morning as I walked late to school. Indeed that is what I needed to do, I affirmed to myself. *Fight life with life!* I should care for myself more. I should laugh. I should remove that scowl from my face. I should stop eating like a pig, shed some weight. I should plait my hair, do some things with it, dress in good clothes. I should use makeup. Images ran through my mind like a reel of film. The thought about makeup made me smile and my spirit lifted. Come on, fight life with life, Doreen. Get that laughter out of the dark corner, air it out in the sun and see how it starts to bloom into color!

Mother, how did you do it?

CHAPTER 17

Riders of night buses are invariably tired or lonely or beaten to submission by harsh realities of life. I was very tired the night I met Joseph. The bus was half empty when I entered and walked down the isle looking for a place to sit. A man, middle aged and well dressed, said as I approached, "Come. Let us sit together here." He stood up to give me the window seat and I obliged. He looked pleased with himself as we exchanged greetings. He smiled.

I heaved a sigh of fatigue and looked out the window. He was no longer of consequence to me and I did not even look at him.

That morning I had dressed in a new dress. I had had it made by a tailor introduced to me by a fellow teacher. I thought I looked good. My teacher friend who I had gone to visit said I looked good. For a whole afternoon, we had sat at a nearby bar drinking beer and eating goat meat, talking about the normal things: other teachers, our neighbors and their lives, how rich or poor they were, how good looking. Who was seducing who with what success. A lot of gossip and laughter and normalcy! The visit had ended at eight in the night.

As I stood waiting for a bus home, fatigue descended upon me although I had not done any tiring work. Where was the happiness

I was looking for? How would I find the laughter I needed? I would have liked to go away somewhere to rest or be with people who did not have to talk about other people and their failings as a way of survival. I needed positiveness in my life! That is the way to laughter! I looked at the people around me waiting for a bus. Older people looked distant, their faces lined with a dignified tiredness. The younger ones chatted with each other, laughing loudly at completely plain things. I realized, almost with a panic that I was alone, alienated, even from the ability to laugh at small and plain things. A nagging passion waiting to be released had wrapped up my soul into a parcel. I thought, desperately: I should write Zima. I should ask him how his marriage was doing. Perhaps I should tell him about Martin and myself. I should release this weight I am dragging around. I could ask him whether men were also afflicted with the common virus of being *normal* by way of spending half the night in bars so that they do not appear henpecked. I should ask him if he knows how to accept normalcy, the step- by- step things to do. Zima was always a practical man, he would probably know just what I needed to do.

When the bus came and I boarded, I was still thinking about Zima and the letter I was going to write. Perhaps he will be honest enough to tell me the truth, I thought. Frankness from Zima is what makes his letters so interesting. It has become a conspiracy of some sorts, because we feel safe to admit the social pretences and lies to ourselves, so that we become spectators (only in the letters) to a life being acted out on stage! We are better friends now, like secret lovers who aren't quite carrying on a love affair. The thought of a love affair made me smile, and I leaned my head on the windowpane, to better savor the feeling of the possibility of being

Zima's lover. I felt a hand, so lightly, on my shoulder.

The man looked at me. He must have been really good looking when he was younger, my mind concluded quickly. His eyes looked younger than the face, more energy radiated from there. His lips formed and then unformed words that he did not speak. Finally he gave up trying to start a conversation, and fumbled in the inside pocket of his jacket, fishing out some photographs. They were photos of paintings; village women clad in colorful clothing, thrashing beans or some kind of corn. Other women were winnowing, pouring seed against the wind from some basket onto the ground. Three women concentrated on the act of removing seed from chaff. There was another painting of a land in limbo, a land threatened by severe drought, of parched earth needing rain. The light was focused on the roots, shriveled and gnarled under the ground, searching for water.

He showed me the photographs one by one, looking at each first before he put them on my hand. He did not explain any thing, he gave no descriptions or history. So I took my time to look for the story the pictures told and he moved closer to share the looking with me. I did not mind, I was content to find preoccupation outside myself.

The photographs were not new. The paper was yellowing and the corners of some had started to fray. As he looked at them with me, with almost equal curiosity, I thought; this man is just an egoist wanting to be spectator of his own work! Or perhaps something he had thought he captured now eluded him, and he was hoping that another eye might pull his own to the point where mystery lay? With these thoughts, I concentrated on the pictures, looking for the meaning, following the bait of my own mind.

The paintings were done in oil, the artist achieving a spectacular harmony between the colors and the subject: the women. The women were almost color itself, brilliant red, yellow and green. I observed the painting for a long time, trying to discover something unique that was expressed in the women's eyes, but I saw only what they were doing. I looked at the land in limbo for a long time, at the roots cutting through stone, wandering through a parched earth so totally blind to their need!

Will the searching ever stop? The effect of the painting created in me a sense of urgency, a kind of unease I could not immediately understand.

"Are you married?" I heard the man ask, drawing me rather violently from the thoughts of the art works.

I was surprised by that change of subject, so I hesitated before I said, "Yes."

"Do you have children?"

"Yes. One," I replied.

He looked past me out the window.

I looked at his face again and thought; he must have been married for as long as he can remember. He looked simply middle aged and closed, a kind of face with the ability to wear a veil of skin. He wore a gold watch, very expensive, I figured. His clothes too looked expensive. His body was lean. His hair had a good measure of white. He could grow a beard, but his face was shaved clean and the tone of his skin told me of a man who had lived well and who knew the value of exercise.

I could never tell what feeling was simmering just under his skin, to prompt questions about my personal life. I thought of Martin, his transparent face that comes alive with every emotion. I loved him best when he was happy and excited, captured by desire, when his face sort of floated in a halo of tenderness. But lately, his capacity for passion had been tamed, or retired to a dark corner, like mine. He was more quiet and mellow now. No, this man was not like Martin at all.

I started to speculate about him. A man who paints women winnowing must be different, special. Or he just saw them as laborers, poor, overworked farmers. May be they were just objects. No, I would see his ego in the painting if they were just objects. He would paint them differently, maybe naked, or almost naked. He would exaggerate some parts of their bodies, like breasts, thighs, eyes or the torso, imposing his lust on those parts. There is always such a thin line between subjectivity and objectivity for the artist, sometimes the two being completely elusive.

Perhaps these were his village aunts he painted, clothing them with color and elegance and determination of spirit. He must have loved them. There was so much sympathy in the rendering. The women seemed to be the anchor of the earth from which they harvested the seed they winnowed, the wind blowing against and around them to carry the chaff away.

Could these women be the subject of his dreams?

He coughed to draw my attention, then said, rather quietly, "I get off at the next stop."

"Oh," I said.

"Come with me. I have something I would like to tell you," he said with hesitation. "I know you do not know me, but, you know, one has to start somehow..." He tried to smile, but it was more a gesture of reassurance than a smile. Then, "we can go for a drink, at a nearby place," he added hurriedly.

It was the dread of a home without Martin that encouraged me to go with him, a certain need to commune with someone outside the society of teachers who made my social circle. I still held the photographs in my hand. He looked at them but did not take them, nor did I give them back. My hesitation encouraged him and he made as if to hold my hand, pleading with his eyes. He looked safe and kind, I affirmed to myself and made a decision.

"Okay, but I will not stay long." He smiled and we hurried off the bus.

We did not go to a nearby bar as he had said. We walked quite a distance from the bus stop. He was completely at ease with walking, relaxed and energetic while I started to pant and struggle with my high-heeled shoes that I never used for walking. He introduced himself simply as Joseph and I said I am Doreen. We spoke little, not having found a common frequency to carry on a conversation. Finally, we arrived at a big, beautiful house surrounded by huge trees.

Two dogs, big and intimidating, came barking from the dark. They gradually toned down to groaning endearingly and mock biting his hands as he petted them.

The house was lighted, but he opened the door with a key, indicating that there was no one to open for him.

"Please come in and sit down," he said and went straight in without waiting for me to sit. I hesitated and remained standing, not being sure whether I should make myself comfortable. I heard the flush of a toilet.

"Oh, please, please, sit down," he said, when he came back, a bit embarrassed. He held my hand, led me to a sofa against the opposite wall from the door. "Please," he said and left me again.

He was much more animated in his house than he was in the bus. He even looked younger as more light came into his eyes and energy into his body. Perhaps the situation in the bus intimidated him. And why did he take a bus instead of driving his car, a Mercedes, which was parked in an open garage by the house?

I sat down on the corner of the sofa, suddenly worried and afraid. Who was this man? Where was the wife? What would she think of me coming home with *her* husband at night? The foolishness of my decision to accompany him dawned on me. Nervously, I wondered if I could conjure up any convincing excuse for coming to her home with her husband just to talk and have a beer! Jesus, I should go, right now! Everything suddenly felt strange and dangerous. How come there was no one in this place? Where were the children, a domestic servant, a relative, anyone?

But the nervousness was only in me. The house was quiet. It gave the ambience of peace. The lighting was pleasant, the furniture scanty. There were many paintings and sketches on the walls. They must have been arranged to achieve a certain impact because of the way light was made to shine on them. I wanted to look at the pictures, but that would show a familiarity that I was afraid to display. So I sat with my back straight, my hands on my laps, like I was readying myself to run. Finally, he came back with two cold Safari beers and glasses and sat down beside me saying,

"Relax. I am an old man living alone."

"I would like to meet your wife," I said, tentatively.

I did not trust that he lived alone in this huge house. He looked a man of status, perhaps a big name in politics or business. It took him some time before he said, "She left me for another man. They do not live in Dar es Salaam."

It took me time also to digest what he had said, the possibilities, and the reasons. He said it so nonchalantly. I wanted to ask why she left, but a gut feeling told me to let that be, for the time being, so I asked, "What about the children?"

"I have two. A girl, Luisa, is a lecturer at the University of Dar es Salaam. She teaches development economics in the Institute of Development Studies. Luisa has such incredible independence of spirit, I have all the sympathy for the man who will marry her, if she ever gets married. She lives with a man, a beautiful young person of mixed race called Wickman. I do not ask her questions, because from the very beginning when she introduced the man to me, she said that their agreement was 'no conditionality', that is the word she used." He shrugged his shoulders, as though to say, 'what can I do'. "I love it when they come for a day or so. They are full of life together.

I have a son too, Fetai, we all call him Fe. He is now a young man studying art in America. We are not on good terms. We quarreled over the phone, so he has chosen not to write for almost three months now. Anyway, I should not burden you with my problems."

He said that with seeming disinterest, throwing the thought away with his hand, as if it was a side issue in his life, a thing of small consequence. It was the feeling reflected on his face that spoke of dissatisfaction and resignation. I immediately noticed the change of mood when he talked about his son.

He spread his hands on the back of the sofa in both directions and let his head fall on it. I sat up to avoid resting my back on his hand. I was about to ask him about the wife again when he said, "Please don't dig me up like a yam. I do not mean any harm in bringing you here."

I sipped the beer and held my peace. It tasted cold and good.

The house was still. Even the dogs outside seemed to have gone to sleep.

I looked around to familiarize myself with the place. The sitting place was big. The furniture was extremely frugal of material, very little wood and cushioning. I compared them with ours at home that were heavy and generous, like small beds. The floor was not carpeted wall to wall as I had seen in rich people's houses. There were three rugs, strategically placed so that the eye did not have to struggle towards the focal points, and those were related to the whole arrangement. The carvings, pottery, paintings and sketches, everything belonged to its place, somehow. This was a beautiful house. Who kept the house for him if the wife had left? Who had this taste?

"What is he like?" The man had a habit of scaring me out of my thoughts!

"Who?"

"Him. Your husband."

I smiled. A light thought flashed through my mind - am I the one to be dug up like a yam? But I let the thought pass and wondered instead what he expected to hear, this quiet and lovely, yes, lovely man left by his wife for another man. What picture of Martin has he drawn in his mind?

"Where is he?" he asked again when I did not immediately respond.

"We live in Kawe," I said and added, "He works with the Ministry of Education."

He kept quiet.

I could have guessed then what he was thinking about. It would have prepared me for what was to come, but at that time, Martin filled my heart so that there was no room for me to look at Joseph and see his need. Later, I realized that my resolve to wake up from the state of self- pity had not, on that day, gone any deeper than the skin. I was just a walking zombie trying hard not to look at my sadness.

"He does not love me anymore because I cannot bear him a boy child. Milika, our daughter, was okay for us at the beginning, before we became normal. Anyway, that is the state of things now."

The confession about him and his wife had become infectious. I felt bad saying those things about us, feeling as though I was betraying Martin, but it was done.

He looked at me with keen interest. His gaze unclothed my privacy, exposing a truth that could perhaps have been safely hidden under the surface of personal everyday life.

He was quiet. He shook his head, but said nothing. Then he laid his right hand gently on mine. It was soft and warm. He rubbed my arm saying, "It is not the end of life."

A hard lump settled in my throat. I tried hard to swallow it. I said, "Ah, its nothing. I don't really care about what he does." My voice sounded broken.

He went to get more drinks. It was getting late but something held me down where I sat. My mind was reluctant to engage itself in the return journey. I think there are times in one's life when everything ceases to be important, when inertia holds time within itself and it matters not whether it is day or night, or whether one is awake or asleep.

After he came back and poured the drinks, he said, "Doreen, you are not alone. Many of us seem to be wandering in this bewildering emotional forest, seeking for direction, a way into the open clearing."

I waited. I did not want to start talking about us again. I think I was afraid of what I would say.

My silence encouraged him to go on. He did feel like talking, like pouring out something he had kept inside the mind for a long time. "I lived with my wife for twenty two years. *Twenty-two!* I tell you, that many years and I thought I loved her. I *believed* I loved her. After she left and I was alone and able to think of our life together, in her absence, then I was not so sure. Did I really love her? Did she love me at all? Can love sustain marriage, bonding the partners in a way that lasts? Suddenly, all the certainty I had felt all these years dissolved into doubts and I could not answer any of the questions I asked myself. Doreen, what sustains marriage in the absence of love? Imagine, I was asking myself these questions after twenty- two years of marriage. It felt so odd!

Then I told myself, okay, Justine, that is her name, was the familiar person I lusted for. That, however did not hold. You know, a man does not experiment with a wife, the mother of his children. He cannot be a naughty, unrestrained man with a woman over whom he exercises authority. So he goes out. It is not true, as most women think, that a man goes out with other women only when he is unhappy at home. No. He does all the proper things to the wife, gets her what she and the children want and need, then he goes out to play, look for fun. He can even fall in love once in a while. Young boys somehow learn that as they grow up, observing it in their elder brothers and fathers and they accept it as the ruling reality of life, as truth. I believed that too."

He went quiet and contemplative. "But if I knew that, if I

believed it, why then would I lust for Justine? For her sensual beauty, her intelligence and sensitivity? And if I did lust for her, then I must have loved her!"

He was still in that forest where familiar ground had surprisingly turned alien. In that we were together friend, Joseph. Yes, like me, he was still in the fog, trying to find his way around a road traveled for twenty- two years without knowing the difference between lust and love, where one ended and the other started. But, there we parted, friend. For me, love ended and lust ended. Normalcy settled in.

Time has allowed me, again, to see that I was wrong. Love did not end, nor did lust. I was being like Great Aunt Mai, I was circling the hurt, I was scaring away the pain. That is why I was failing to accept normality and be happy in it.

Sitting there with Joseph beside me, hearing him talk, I realized how life was always planned for men: 'This is what is done before there is a wife; this is what is done when there is a wife; this is what is done when there are children; this is what is done when there is love in marriage; this is what is done when there is no love; and this is...." Well, well, well, what do women do? Love their men and lust for others or love them faithfully and never look at others?

I imagine my sister-in-law asking me that question. She is my teacher, and I am a thin, shy pupil sitting at the back of the class, looking down at the plain, used face of the desk so that the teacher will not discover the fear and the uncertainty in my eyes and pounce on me demanding an answer. But the teacher seeks me out. Yes, Doreen Seko, what do women do?

My heart throbs within my chest. I look fearfully around the class like a coward. Some pupils are already giggling, waiting for my answer. I say, quietly, as if my vocal chords are cobwebs, 'they weave fantasies around their lives. They live by those fantasies until a little wind blows through the cracks, then they merge inwards, collapsing into themselves like a sand castle, falling at the feet of their mighty men. The very courageous ones, the outrageous ones, go out and engage in timid play. Then there are those who seek free space, those are marked as deviant and sometimes mad.' I imagine the class breaking into laughter, and me, taking cover under the desk to hide from the possible wrath of ...

"That is the glorious mirror of patriarchy," I heard him say.

"What is that?" I asked, shaken again into the present. I had never heard the idea before.

"Oh, you don't know what patriarchy means?" He smiled ruefully." Every woman should know it," he said.

He explained the meaning of patriarchy. "It is a social system which has defined how men and women will relate in all spheres of life, including private life, right down to the way we love and have sex. It has determined how a father, brother, husband, uncle will treat the woman- the wife, sister, mother, and daughter related to them. It is an ideology that has given the man the authority to decide, to act, to give or withhold, to access or retain anything, really, almost everything. It is complex. It is a web in which, ultimately, even those privileged can become victims... like myself." He stopped.

I was agape. "A system! You mean... who designed it? What is ideology anyway?"

He laughed, Joseph laughed at me that day. A hearty, racy laugh that transformed his face.

"Why do you laugh?"

"Because you make me laugh." And he laughed some more.

"Oh, God," he said and picked up empty beer bottles and went for more.

"You don't want to say it, but it must be the men," I said as he came back.

"What about the men?" he asked.

"It must be them who designed such things as system and ideology and patriarchy! Such *evil*. You know what I call it, I call it the spider's web. You have now given it another name. Men must be the spider who spins the web from the secretions of its own stomach in order to capture others for it to eat! Oh, the cruelty of it!"

"Wait, wait, wait. We are all in it. All of us, women and men. The enemy is the system, not the men. Look at me, I am as much a victim as you with the boy child thing."

I was not convinced about that, but I knew hardly anything about it. I mean, I knew how it *felt* to be in that system. It felt like itching, an all body itch. But I did not know the cause of the itch. I decided there and then to learn from this man who knew so much and who could talk to me without restraint. I would learn. All these victims! mother, Godbless, Martin....

"And why is it that people have not thought of changing it, tearing it down like one demolishes a haunted house in order to build another?" I asked Joseph. I was angry (and a little drunk?) and slowly slipping into a state of emotional laxity.

"Don't worry, it is decaying already. It is weakened to its very foundations because situations that sustained it have changed so much. You know, girls are going to school and some are discovering that they have rights. Women are wielding power; they are lawyers, industrialists, professors; they are accessing and generating information that has influence over others. Women are owners of property, depending less and less on the benevolence of male relations. Now women are voting men out of power. They are making decisions about their lives. Look at me and Justine... so much is happening now. It may seem small and inconsequential, but the foundations are being shaken, the power base is eroding and before we know, *pam*, real change will start to be seen.

But you know what is really shaking the earth? You know what will finally throw patriarchy off board totally; it is society allowing and *accepting* that, yes, a man can *need* another man and a woman can *need* another woman as intimate partners. It is society saying, yes, these alternatives can co-exist with the norm, the woman-man norm, they can make a family and can raise children. That, in my opinion, is the beginning of real change in the organization of human society. You see, because history is made by man - I am being one here- because history is created by man in his struggle to adapt to and tame the environment, spiritual and material, it has a way of going full circle, then finally coming round again to the beginning. Once upon a time there was a woman and there was a man. They lived their independent lives in the world until the concept of private property gained currency and a structure called family became the cornerstone....It is about time history came round.. ."

"I swear to you, I don't understand anything you have said. I should not lie. I understood a bit of what you said about patri-something, about *that* system, because I have seen things happen in it. This other thing is too confusing for me. You know, I am a primary school teacher," I said, admitting to myself that it is better to show my ignorance than to hide it.

He laughed, loudly again, until his chest shook and his eyes filled with tears, showing me his good set of teeth and making me feel foolish. He said, looking at me, "Doreen, you are a beautiful, intelligent, inquisitive and very sensitive woman. You really are... and more." He rose quickly, disturbed by something, and went away.

I believe, from that moment something opened in my mind, like a ray of light pushing out the darkness that had clouded my understanding of life. I knew, definitely, I would come back to the huge house surrounded with trees many more times. I needed to understand the workings of the system that had fed us with poison, which had impaled us with pain and blind suffering. I needed to understand the other things he talked about. I wanted to know the man.

The night was aging when he grudgingly took me home in his Mercedes Benz. I felt light and happy to have met him. Before I got out of the car, he said, "I would like to be a friend to you, Doreen. I would like that very much." The initial nervousness was back in his voice, the uncertainty.

He saw my hesitation and almost in desperation said, "I mean, we could be friends, you know, talk about things, be together sometimes. I ... do not mean anything else," he said. I shook my head in agreement and opened the door.

"How ...where can I get you? I mean..."

"I teach at Kawe Primary School," I told him, not knowing how to get out of this situation, yet not wanting to run away from this man called Joseph, who I felt, needed a friend as much as I did.

That night, alone in bed, I resolved to bring Martin from his wanderings to the warm hearth of home. It was not his fault, I resolved. It was the fault of this system that taught him how to be a man, that gave conditions for being a man, giving him criteria which did not apply. It was his relatives, the keepers of tradition who played with his mind, toyed with his heart until Martin thought the desire to have a male child was *his*, that his wonderful girl child who he loved was inadequate qualification for acceptance into the cult of manhood!

A consciousness, playing at the edge of decision, already indicated that I should look for this child so desired by him and his family and give him to Martin. Oh, yes I will, because I love him. Isn't that what Aunt Mai said? Look around you, carefully, and give your man the child he craves for! It is women who look for a child, not men!

That good old woman wisdom which had thrown my mind in total disarray had been used as a strategy to beat down the male order! Honestly! A woman is a dangerous guerrilla fighter. Fight life with life, my mother had shown me all the time. Smart women! Oh, I am so thick, how could I not even have sensed it?

My resolve acted on my mind like warm, soapy water acts on greasy dishes. It cleaned away all the resentment I had accumulated. When Martin came back from his trip, he found a happy and welcoming Mrs. Patrick. He was infected by my mood, as I talked on end about my work and Milika's school progress. He stayed home that night and we kind of tried to talk about our life.

It was such a long time since we had dared to venture into the quicksand that our life had become.

CHAPTER 18

J oseph came to school to see me a week after we had met and I agreed to meet him again. We had lunch at a tourist hotel by the sea. He just wanted to know me more, so I talked, mostly, and he became a sponge, absorbing the history of my family as I poured it into him. He came to know my brother Godbless, about him and mother, about the consuming desire to have a father who did not want him. I told him about Great Aunt Mai and Uncle Simbo, about grandmother and grandfather and what they did to my mother, long ago when she became pregnant with Godbless. Joseph listened quietly, looking at me intently as I shone in his attention.

In most of my life, I have listened to men talk, say things to me that they believed in or did not like; things they did or planned to do and how. They have wanted me to listen but not comment or give my opinion and I have obliged. I became privy to their dreams and how they will realize them, starting with Godbless, who had dreams I identified with as if they were mine, all the way into adulthood, with Zima who planned his family with me in it, even Martin, the headmasters of the schools I have taught in, the various men friends I have had. They have always talked *to* me. Joseph made me wonder if the men ever thought that I could add anything of value to their plans, dreams, opinions; and if they didn't, then why would they talk to me at all?

I have observed that while women tend to talk with each other, men talk to women; they tell them things. Men think about what is best for women, they generate ideas which women internalize. Men create a life for women to live in and enjoy themselves and this makes women get attached to them. I suppose that is how a woman's voice is killed, gently, so that there is no resistance or even complaint when they find themselves voiceless before men.

I talked little about my mother. I have known her more sensually, instinctually, so that the language with which to describe her is not verbal. I have felt her emotionally, touched or smelled her or seen her sad or happy and this sensual communication has evoked from me some knowledge of who she could be. But then, what I would talk about would be more about me than about her, as I related to her, day by day through the warmth and smell of her body; the grip of her hand on me; the sharpness of her voice; the sadness in her eyes; the ring of her laughter; it would be my interpretation of the influence of her being on me. That is what I told Joseph when he asked me to talk more about my mother. He accepted my explanation, was satisfied with the little I had said.

And finally, before I pushed him to ask me again, I talked about Martin.

Words were hard in coming. He supported his head on his left hand, pivoted on the table, as if to say he was ready to wait until the words came. The lunch dishes had been cleared. He had convinced me to take a cold beer and his silence was like a soft song.

"I stand at the precipice in my relations with Martin," I started.

This was really the first time someone was anxious to hear me talk regarding my feelings about Martin. Zima couldn't stand it, members of the River Pebbles Club preferred the gossip to my own story, my sister-in-law scorned the love I felt for him. As this was the first time someone showed real interest, I took another sip of beer to brace myself. My own thoughts had started moving in circles in my own mind, so it was a relief to talk to Joseph. I looked at his face, in a way pleading for his patience and understanding. Around us instrumental music played softly and the sea, in the distance, was calm.

"I have never loved a man the way I loved Martin. He churned my insides, made me courageous, rebellious, and vulnerable. With him, I have learned how to be patient, how to wait and persevere. I have learned to communicate, to obey and to trust my daemon. Living with and loving Martin has taught me faith and prayer and how to accept defeat. He still is everything beautiful and sensitive to me..."

I described our meeting, the first outing and those strange struggles with my daemon. I told him about our wedding, the period of dreams, how he vibrated with utmost beauty. "Then something happened and took him away, yanked him violently from the warmth of the home we had created together. Now, he only comes to sleep."

My throat was parched by a hot dryness, so I took large gulps of beer to push it down into the silence of the stomach. Joseph was fingering his glass, looking into it, the beer hardly touched.

I continued, "Now, I look at the inside of my heart and I see the pedestal on which I had put him empty and forlorn. Echoes of the love he showed me he was capable of giving, the possibilities for laughter and wild ecstasy haunt me like a bad dream. What do I do?"

He was totally quiet.

"Joseph," I called his attention back to me. He looked away from my face.

I stopped talking.

The conversation that followed was about teaching. He talked a bit about his work, especially when he was in France.

I did not go back to school that day.

Joseph came again, but it was exam time so I did not have time to go out with him. A letter from Godbless a week after exams forced me to see Joseph at his house.

Godbless was getting married, but more than that, he had finally confronted his father. The most desired and wanted person in his life!

He wrote; "...*I had to do it sister. My fiancé wanted to know who my father was and I had to tell her my story. Why shouldn't I? What child is born into this world without a father? It was then I decided not to get married without settling the matter with him! Mother refused completely to do it for me. "He denounced you when he chose the safety of silence," she said. "He gave both of you up, you and your sister Doreen, when his father's wish became more important, stronger than your lives. What do you want me to tell him now, after all these years?" You know mother, when she says, 'let me be', she has concluded everything. There will be no more action. So I went to Mati, his oldest daughter, and told her, "Look Mati, I am your brother, real brother. I am getting married and I would like my sister to be with my mother, now that Doreen can not come." Mati did not believe me. She refused completely. I said, okay, I will come and ask your parents to give you permission to do it. They know. I went to her house, with a friend of mine. I had to tell him everything before he did it. This friend talked really nicely to the mother, about how I want to settle down and that with Doreen not being around, we are asking for Mati to take her place as a sister. The friend was really good, but you should have seen how the mother got very disturbed. I remained calm. The friend was quite calm too. The next day we agreed that he goes to the father to get his approval before mother herself comes to present an official request. That is when the man went wild with anger! That is also when Mati got very surprised that I was not lying and started to ask how come they never heard of it. You know how gossip never gets to the real subject! Finally, the secret that has never been a secret came out...The whole village is talking things I never knew about, how our father loved mother and almost killed his father who had blood pressure...I thought mother would be very angry with me but she was not. You know, sister, I do not need my father any more now...My fiancée is a beautiful girl, she told me that it was better she heard it from me than through gossip... I am very, very proud of her and you will be proud of her too...*

I wanted to share the contents of the letter with Joseph. I wanted him to talk about patriarchy again. I wanted someone else to affirm to me that Godbless has and will survive.

I was surprised anew at a man living alone, in overalls this time, and I asked him how he managed. "There is a woman who cleans and cooks every day. I do not need much, a sandwich here, something small there. Then there is a man who takes care of the garden, and another who stalks the night to ensure my safety."

"You arrange everything in here yourself? You select everything?"

"It *is* my house, you know," he said, irritably. "I don't need someone to tell me where to put my paintings, or how."

His mood was rash, as if preoccupied with something else. I must have interfered with his work although he acted happy to see me. "I will not stay long," I said.

"Give me a few minutes, I will be ready to be with you one hundred percent," he said, brightening up a bit.

He went away for what seemed like forever. I decided to ask him what he does with the paintings that seemed to occupy him almost all the time. Then finally, he came back without the overalls, carrying two beers. We settled down and took our drinks. He sighed deeply. I recognized, with almost a sense of guilt, that I felt so peaceful in his house.

"Will you marry again," I asked him.

"No. Not at this time," he said, shaking his head. "I can not go through it again. I can live with a woman perhaps, but even such women are not to be found. And you, Doreen ...are already tied to Martin ..."

I was flattered and embarrassed. The image of Martin loomed in my mind like a warning signal and I thought it better not to continue the subject. I wanted to tell him that Godbless had broken the rules by openly claiming his father, by stating to the world that there is no child born to a woman alone without a father. I wanted him to know that Godbless had finally claimed his place in the order of things. I wanted to give him the letter to read, but he looked sad and pensive and vulnerable, so I kept quiet instead and drank my beer.

Then he said, "You asked me if I will marry again. Frankly, I am afraid. What difference shall I bring to the second marriage? I am afraid I will want the same privileges, so I will be the same man, but one living in fear of being left again.

You know, a man gets used to a woman like he gets used to his house, that place he calls home. *A woman is a man's home.* When he enters the house, he expects food, a place to rest, and some comfort.

A man expects those things without subjecting himself to a lot of thought about the woman who makes those things happen. A man *knows* that he is the source of the food and comfort and that he deserves all he asks for. He thinks little about the woman, until that woman leaves and takes the restful atmosphere and the comfort. Only then, the meaning of wife settles in... and he discovers he is not the source of much."

There we were again, in full agreement. I could have clapped, but I only said, "That's true."

"Women are survivors," he continued. "Justine was a good wife to me. A very good wife. She let me be. She never directly questioned much of what I did. After she left, I honestly did not know what to believe. She had prepared my meals, washed my clothes, accompanied me to every party that required me, as diplomat, to be with my partner, she had posed for my paintings, many of them. She had done all that without complaints. She was with me nightly in my bed and ... well, we had no problems with sex. Justine was so sensuous and her body so beautiful I could not see her naked and not be aroused. I never thought we had any problem until I found out, accidentally, that she had had an affair with a man for several years!

What is it she did not like?" he asked, shaking his head in that desperate admission of defeat for a runner who thinks he is a winner until the end of the race when he finds out he is the last to arrive.

He seemed to have risen above self- pity. He had lived with his ego in this house, alone, for long enough to see himself in the mirror and to recognize the image of a man who had fueled rebellion, perhaps unknowingly, in a woman who had loved him for years, had seen her love taken for granted, trampled upon until the source itself dried up. Was it when she decided to love another man, decided to leave this one, with his art, his money, house, prestige and all?

Godbless, in his letter had said that Sebastian's wife had left him. Regarding that, mother had said that the wife's leaving was not a problem, they will return her to the man in due course. It was the man Godbless had unsettled, to which Godbless said he had no regret.

Two women, two roads.

"How did you find out?" I asked.

He looked at me and beyond me. I could see that his mind was still held by the elusiveness of his question: What is it she did not like?

What is it Martin did not like when he chose to love another woman?

Marriage is a house of mirrors!

He seemed to be weighing whether to answer me or not, whether to expose the rawness of his pain. He looked at me again for a long moment, then he said hoarsely, "I found the man's letters in her handbag that I never saw her use. I don't even remember what I was looking for. She was not home."

I kept quiet. I waited for him to continue talking. "I could not resist reading them, but once I started, my hands started trembling and I started to sweat. It took me so long to read just two letters."

I could imagine how he felt, a surprise meeting with an enemy. Unprepared, unguarded, unarmed, while the enemy held a weapon, sharp as a dagger and directed at his heart. I would also sweat and tremble and fear for my life. Sometimes it is better not to know, better to keep guessing, because imagination, guided by the inherent instinct for survival will become sympathetic to the heart.

He stood up tiredly. He walked as if he had covered tens of miles on foot, as if the load he carried was getting too heavy for him. I regretted coming to his house on such a day as this, but at the same time told myself that he needed another person, another body to relate to, not music, not painting.

He went into one of the rooms and emerged with some letters in his hand. He gave them to me without a word and then sat down and drank some more beer. I read pieces of them silently.

"...Magic. That is the name of our love. That is how we were made to be: one in a pact that none of us was party to or had any choice about. Two letters in a mantra. Two words in a magic chant.... The measure of my love for you, in all manners of it, could only be made by a person holding the two of us together, like a yoke to a pair of draught animals, an axle to two turning wheels. Then that person would be able to know the throb of my flesh that craves for you; the awe that shakes my being every time I contemplate how fate gently placed you in my arms and continues to bring you to me time and time again despite every hurdle, every impossibility...." It was a long letter full of emotion, full of desire and wonderment *"...how does anyone love in the turmoil of the wave that crashes and smashes and rises to smash and crash once again?..*, the longing and torment *"... what is this torment that throws this soul into the depths of sunfire?"* the plea *"...oh, come to me, come to my rescue Justine, earth mother!"*

I felt drenched by the passion, the strength of it. She surely had to go to him, she had to decide whether to go to his rescue or let the man burn down to ashes! I felt for the man as I read through the pages, how he longed for someone else's wife, how he had sunk, whole, body and soul, into passion for this woman! Love, the osmotic force that recognizes no physical boundaries, that defies morality, the power that crushes, with its heel, the stubborn head of human superiority. Well, the lover must have known, in this life threatening contest with his ego, that it will need a love so deep, so total, to move her to him.

In another shorter letter, the lover wrote, *"... I pray for us. I pray that we may see the beauty of God in our selves, in all that we do and think, in the force, oh, the indulgent force that brings us together. I pray with all the power in my frame of flesh and bone, that we treat this love with reverence and humility ..."*

I sat there and imagined the pain of Joseph having to witness another man's desperate love for his own wife. And in the end, what it meant to meet such truth. That must have cut him like a knife.

He shook his head disbelievingly and sipped his beer. "I never beat her, not once, not even in the heat of anger she had fanned. I bought her the most expensive clothes and jewelry. I took time to think of what she may want, even considering her moods at the time. I pampered her with gifts, well, because it pleased me to see her excited and loving.... I never really seriously quarreled with Justine. I just don't understand!" he said, shaking his head and looking at me, his face full of shock. "What do women look for in their men?" he asked.

"I know what women look for. You want to know?" I asked him.

He looked at me, stared hard at me, then shook his head up and down, slowly, and said, very quietly, "Yes, Doreen. I want to know."

"You know, Joseph, the shame of it is this: men do not *look* at women much. They project their expectations on the women and that is what they see. The actual woman eludes them. Let me tell you what women look for in their men: they look for reciprocity; women look for appreciation for their contribution to the life of the whole household, for material, spiritual and emotional contribution which they give every single hour of their being woman, wife and mother. And you know, that is a very simple thing- recognition in form of kindness, understanding and sympathy sometimes. Women look for sensitivity, so that she is not looked upon as a willing beast of burden, a 'loved' slave. And yes, women look for men who will *love* them."

He remained silent for a long time. "You are right, Doreen. Of course, you are right. It is so interesting you say that. We so often think we are appreciating when we provide material things, comfort - a car, a house, money. When we are kind and respectful of them as mothers of our children, we consider it a duty finished. Yes, the shame of it, as you put it, is that, that is how we are raised, men and women. That's the tragedy really."

We both kept quiet and sought intimacy and safety in the night that was creeping in. Both of us saw that there was something wrong somewhere. Suddenly it felt as if life was threateningly deep and complex. We were just floating in its powerful current, in a force we could not tame. Is that why we try to put form to it, shape some kind of order to tame the life force too big for us to contain? The laws, the conditions, traditions and customs, the systems. Patriarchy! Now, look how we fret as we struggle to outwit the very conditions we set for ourselves! How we strive to release ourselves from our own trap!

What do women look for in their men?

I looked at Joseph. In spite of the pain, I saw a man at peace with his situation. He had entered the ring of battle, between himself and love for his wife from another man, an antagonist as big as Goliath. I saw the wrath he vented on himself for not knowing, for not having seen a love for another man growing in his partner's heart. That anger, becoming the weapon to kill his desire for the woman now gone from his reach. Well, certainly, he had been beaten, but he had survived.

He went to the far wall of the room and took from the wall a framed photograph of a handsome young boy of sixteen or so. He gave it to me and said, "My son, Fe." He sat down with me and we looked at the photograph together. The son was a younger version of him, but more rounded. The eyes had a penetrating, open gaze. He was bare -chested when the picture was taken. The shoulders, the sparsely fleshed chest, the nipples, prominent like pencil points and the persistent gaze made the boy at once strong and determined in character, and at the same time vulnerable. We looked at him a long time.

"He is my pride and joy, but he does not want to *see* that. When his mother left, he got so angry with me. 'How could you let her go to another man?' he asked in fury. 'What did you do to her to make her go away?'

I had no answers for him. I did not know what I had done to make Justine leave. He could not see my desperation and my pain. He said I mistreated his mother, that all I cared for, all I loved was my work and later, my art. He accused me of neglecting them."

He spoke softly, helplessly but I could see he was in control of his pain. Time had allowed him distance from it so that he could bear it without breaking.

He said, "Sometimes this boy eludes my understanding. He has these insights into issues that are too advanced for his age! I mean, what does he know of neglect when he has not been responsible even for his food? But...," he shook his head again.

"He went to stay with his grandmother in the village once and came back with this concept of woman, that, at that time, I found rather naïve or perhaps innocent. He talked of the intimacy women have with the earth, about men's dependency on them, about how strong women are. 'But we impoverish them with our demands, we overuse them in our selfishness,' he had said with passion.

I was surprised at his thinking. He had just completed form four, too young to be thinking like that! I had asked him, quite fascinated, 'What gave you the idea? Women are not passive creatures, certainly. They know very well what they want. They can determine the direction of their lives.'

'*Agh*, sometimes they forget themselves,' he said. 'They think nurturing others is their mission on earth,' he had said with impatience.

Well, in order to discuss this with him, I had to force myself to get over the fact that he was just a child. I had to admit that he was capable of serious thought. Then I was actually able to look at his point of view. I didn't think, and I still don't think that men are as insensitive to women as Fe claimed. You see, Doreen, men do see the dichotomy that women are tied to, as producers of children and also caretakers of their welfare. Women have no choice in this because the offspring *must* survive! They harbour a natural desire to nurture that which came from their own flesh. It happens without even thinking. Men know this. And I suspect, instinctively, the man knows that the woman is *trapped* by this dichotomy. The man knows that a woman cannot abandon the responsibility of nurturing the offspring without getting blamed. Shame on her, for abandoning her own child, we will all scream! We will not ask for the father, we will not want to know his role in all this. If it is a girl, we will not go running to find out who made her pregnant before we heap blame on her first. We will have no sympathy. It is because men see motherhood in their minds. That is why it is easily considered of less importance in comparison to other issues - like education, the economy... We talk, talk, but with little action. A woman suffers for it, she suffers for a natural urge to ensure the survival of the species! The boy observed this dichotomy. He started dealing with it by writing a poem that he pinned on the studio wall as if to guide him in his painting. I think his quest for an answer is still on. The poem is still pinned to the wall.

"Can I see it?" I ventured.

He hesitated. He did not want to rise again and bring out yet another thing that pricked his already tender heart, but he did. He came back with two pieces of paper. The boy had painted around the poem as if to frame it with a certain color and image.

"It was still rough, the poem, still in the process of evolution, still fighting with form and the quest for answers about what he had seen," Joseph said, as if to appeal for a fair criticism. I read, slowly: *Grandmother & I*

"Once, grandmother said
it is in the nature of woman to bleed...

I immediately felt resistance, an instinctive refusal of that reality. Why should it be so? Joseph saw my reaction and encouraged me to read it to the end.

To groan with pain
grind her teeth...

She said, the source of the river dried up
when they starved her center
Now, the riverbed is scorched and parched
the stones burn like her own ache
where her bones meet.

She cannot weep anymore.
or cry out her pain to the world
because there have been tears
 of molten ash
that etched on her a map older than her being
where history has in bold face
names she was known to have before
and those she will have tomorrow.
She is afraid of looking tomorrow in the eye
because she is uncertain of being anew.
She said, it is in her then only to bleed, giving,
until she stands dry like lumbered wood
to be a woman.

I pleaded,
grandmother, sing the song of the inner chamber. Sing!
Her mouth etched a defiance of will
She will not speak
of places treasured like forbidden trysts.
where her Soul dwells
Not until I churn her hurt
with the voice of
the war chant.

"It is too sad, it makes me feel helpless. It sounds as if the woman knows her situation but is helpless, almost unwilling to change it," I said.

"It is possible Fe thought that too. He also saw that women do have a secret life that almost runs like a current beneath the surface of their lives. A kind of survival strategy they are unwilling to publish to the world...," Joseph said, reflecting for a while, then, " I would not have guessed that Justine had a passionate love affair while she lived with me, I could not have known she would actually leave me at any time... so...it is still incredible that he saw an aspect of a woman's life that I had not bothered to see."

Current beneath the surface of their lives....

I thought of my mother and wondered what we saw of her, what the world saw of her, how much of her life she let the world see. Are women driven to this or is it just in their nature, as the boy thought? How much is Aunt Mai's survival strategy open knowledge?

"It is still very frightening," I said, still thinking of my mother. "In the end, after being like lumbered wood, women have no life to show, even to themselves! At some point even the inner life atrophies. Why not just rebel from the very beginning?"

"That is precisely what the boy was trying to understand. Why don't women rebel against servitude and the very subtle oppression from the male order? Sing out the song of the inner chamber, as Fe put it?" he said.

"Justine did... finally," I said, and for the first time saw her action as being motivated by determination for her own survival, separate from what she felt for Joseph or the lover. Justine did it for herself!

Joseph was quiet, thinking. I asked him, "Do you blame Justine for leaving you?"

It took a long time before he said, "It would be hypocrisy to say I did not. I blame her for emptying my life of meaning, for taking away the solid foundation in my life that I always thought was created by me. I cannot help blaming her, feeling betrayed, and yes, abandoned," he said, quietly.

"Men!," I exclaimed, quite involuntarily. I was reacting to a sense of unfairness implied in his blame of Justine.

"Isn't that what you feel for Martin," he shot back at me. Don't you feel betrayed and abandoned?" He sounded irritated. Then immediately, he said, "I know, I know. I am sorry. The hurt is still fresh, Doreen, I do not know how to touch it without hurting, without smarting."

We both kept quiet after that, each of us wanting to escape a terrible truth in our lives, finding easy refuge in our drinks.

When he started talking again, the irritation was gone. "I must admit that Fe's position is very radical. I hope he will not change as he grows older. I really hope so," he said.

"Do you expect age to change him ?"

"Well, one never knows. If he matures in that strain of thought, he will be a happier man, knowing that the woman he loves has a right to sing the song of the inner chamber, and in so doing leave him anytime. He will be a better lover, a better husband that way...Perhaps that is what is needed to keep partners on guard. I do not want him to be like me," he said.

I took the poem and re-read it. He gave me time to finish, then he said, "The difference between him and me is, he sees things with his *heart*, he feels deeply. My eye is cerebral, it rationalizes. I must admit I was filled both with pride and awe. He was only a young boy, just a child in terms of experience."

Joseph smiled, briefly, enjoying the respite that memory offered.

"Fe said he would paint the concept," he continued. "I did not argue with him. I was sure he would understand life better as he grew up. I stayed with him in the studio and watched him paint. I marveled at the sharpness of his colors, the passion he poured on that canvas, trying so hard to bring to life those women and the work they did. He wanted to bring justice to their work and their world. He agonized over how he could respect their position and yet liberate them from that yoke. He went back to it over and over again! I felt humbled somehow. For the first time, his passion and dedication opened a window in my brain that let me *see* a part of him that was turbulent and restless. He made me see what he *could* be. He has so much to offer, so much passion within him, so much power and ability to give! I felt such an acute love for him, there in the studio. It was painful. All I wanted to do was hug him and tell him that things will be okay, that one day that situation of women will change...But I did not hug him ...I was afraid he would push me away. The photographs of women I showed you were of his work."

"Not only the women will survive, Joseph, even the young ones, those who are struggling hard to escape the trap of the spider's web," I said.

He sighed. I could see a certain humility in his eyes, an admission of something he had finally understood.

"I love him. I love him very much, but I don't know how to show him," he said quietly, resignedly.

We sipped our drinks silently. He was going through fire and I could not help him come through in any other way than to be here with him. It was his journey, I was only a bystander witness. I kept quiet to allow him counsel with his heart.

So I tried to suppress the feeling of urgency to leave that started creeping on me. The letter in my pocket was no longer important. It can wait until another day when he is less immersed in sorrow. How shall I get home, I wondered silently. Martin might already be home. I looked at him. His eyes were closed, as if in sleep, but his body was taut with tension.

He said, his eyes still closed "He used to write poems to his mother since he was small. I never knew he wrote poetry until I found them together with the letters of his mother's boyfriend." He recited:

'A mother is someone
who shares your hopes and dreams
she will help with the future
if someone says who is a mother
answer with a proud voice
a mother is someone in my heart.'

He asked, "Where was I in the world of this child? What did his mother do to him which I did not?"

He was angry, but with himself, for missing out on things that eluded him, even now. "I mean, what was I supposed to do? Eh, tell me, what," he asked, fervently, bewildered. "My responsibility was to feed the whole family, clothe them and give them everything they needed. I used to change his wet diaper when he was a baby! I considered it my duty as a good father and husband. *Agh, bwana we.*"

The house became completely quiet, as if in audience to this drama. He sighed heavily. "I am lost," he said.

I could not resist it any longer. Looking at my watch I said, "I must go." I was shocked to realize that it was approaching ten in the night. There would be no buses to Kawe! "I must go," I said again, almost in panic.

"I will take you home," he said, calmly.

"When? I want to go now!" I said in full panic.

He stood up like an obedient child and came to me where I sat and extended his hand for me to stand up. "The last thing I want to do is make you angry or afraid," he said quietly, still holding my hand and standing very close to me. "I will take you home," he said, "but do me one favor. Please kiss me." And he offered himself for kissing.

My impulse was to run, but he still held my hand, tugged at my hand when I tried to move away. It is not that I did not want to kiss him, brush his lips with mine without tarrying long enough to feel drawn in, but that something in me signaled danger, warning me not to walk into quicksand.

"Please, Doreen, don't push me away. Take me, encourage and comfort me. Please," he pleaded, almost in a whisper. He looked tired, haggard, like a person bereaved. He closed his eyes.

"Doreen, please, don't push me away now."

And I did not run. I did not move. I was rooted to the spot with a pulsing heart as he put his arms around me and kissed me instead. Kissed me in that incomprehensible way that is like wanting to merge into the other, dissolve into the other and be one. I lost touch with time, not knowing how long we stood there. After that, he held on to my hug saying, "I wish you did not have to go... but

I know, I know," he said hurriedly as I started to disengage from the embrace.

He took me home.

I think that was the day my life completely changed. Doreen Seko emerged while Mrs. Doreen Patrick also lived. So I got fresh energy from Joseph to see life with a brighter light. I became a better teacher to my pupils in school, because my mind would be with them, with their problems and the insecurities they experienced with learning. I was finally able to rise from the depths, to be spirited enough to seduce friendship in Milika. I was able to see when she was disturbed by something even when she ran out to play without talking about it. I started telling her my feelings about those things she did which made me happy and those that made me upset. She understood immediately and said that sometimes she got angry too when nobody wanted her and dada pretended to be busy. We found moments of enjoyment when we could talk to each other. "Mama, should I tell?"

"Yes, tell."

"There are times I want to cry when you leave me alone with *dada*. And you don't eat with me and *baba* does not eat with me."

The shock of finding out that beneath the carefree mask, there was a person wanting to cry! Oh, the assumptions I had made because I was too immersed in my own problems to *see* the child. How very easy it could be to destroy a life! But before I could recover from the impact of that knowledge and think of how to say sorry, she was telling me more.

"Mama, did you tell *dada* to give me milk every day? I don't like milk. Is it true you will be angry and beat me if I don't drink milk? Is it true?"

"I will never beat you, truly, but your bones need milk to grow," I said, carefully trying to remove the lies from the authority of dada, the angel of the house, almost the pillar, but insisting that milk must be taken.

"Mama, will you take me with you sometimes when you go out? Like when I have done all my maths? Will you?"

I started going out with Milika, visiting places and sometimes shopping in the city.

My life with Martin became more amicable. I made him my friend, defining how much to demand, learning not to expect much, and most importantly, slowly refusing to be hurt by him. When he traveled with the girl, I could ask about her without feeling any anger or jealousy. He was surprised and actually taken aback. I told him that I had accepted that what he offered me emotionally was all that he could offer. I no longer strived to demand love that was not forthcoming from him.

He stayed home more often. Millika became happy again and he shared the school work with her. Often he came home early so that Milika could do her homework with him.

And what happened with that resolve to bring the victim of patriarchy back to the hearth? A way will come, I told myself. I needed more patience and time.

I continued to be a social missionary giving free services to any relative marrying or baptizing a child. I was finally learning my lessons, I was fighting life with life, and so I figured, I would find a lot of time within this framework to meet Joseph.

I wrote Zima regularly. I came to appreciate, infinitely, the lesson that love given and not taken can turn into something awful. Zima responded promptly, expressing great surprise that I had learned to paint. He wanted to know how it happened and how I got the skills and whether I would be teaching the subject in school. Was I thinking of transferring the River Pebbles Club to Kawe, because that is the legacy I had left behind, creating things from rubble, creating happiness from solidarity. Women teachers and even the men talk about me all the time. He said that my letters had become full of hope for the future and that from them he could picture me happy and laughing.

I accepted Joseph into my heart. I did not know exactly how this heart had given up any part of the space that was filled to the edges with love for Martin. I did not know where it would lead me. I was scared by the thought that I could find love in my heart for two men.

CHAPTER 19

His house became my second home. In his studio I learned that loneliness is not a state of being alone, without people, but the inner state of being idle or feeling incomplete.

He taught me how to paint. He said, "Doreen, look at it this way-art is a human expression, and if you are human, you have the capacity for it- any kind of art, not necessarily painting. This is why kindergarten pupils create fantastic art."

I could not refuse to try, and when I looked at the paint as if it had teeth that would bite me if I touched it, he said, "Don't *see* color; *feel* color- first with your hands, dip your hand into the tin."

It was like teaching a child to walk. It took my mind away from everything. It put expectation into my life. I waited for the opportunity to go back to the studio, to handle paint, to hold a brush. "Imagine you are a choir master," he said, " then relax your hands as if you are directing a choir. Don't hold a brush like a kitchen knife."

"What do I paint? My mind is blank, I don't know what to do with the brush!" I panicked, I wanted to learn to paint and I had no image, no picture!

He kept quiet, as if he had not heard. He was my teacher for goodness sake! He was supposed to tell me what to do. He was completely absorbed in his own work. I put the brush back on the plate and slumped on a chair. He walked past me and went out. I could have cried. I went back to the brush again, but nothing came, my hand felt stiff, I could not direct any choir. He came back with two beers, put them on the windowsill, opened one and started drinking. I looked at him, and out of pure frustration, my eyes welled with tears.

"Paint it," he said.

"Paint what? I asked, angry, a big lump in my throat.

"Paint what you are feeling right now. Come on, take that brush and go," he said.

Frankly, I did not know that I would be able to do anything when I unwillingly lifted the brush from the plate of paint. But I did. It had no name or even shape. Later he said, "Engineers, cartographers, even illustrators are artists who make definite shapes. Fine artists make impressions."

That is how I learned to paint. The strange images that appeared on canvas looked alien even to me. Sometimes I felt guilty for wasting expensive paints but he encouraged me by saying, "What value do you want to give your presence in my life?" I understood.

I went home and started drawing with Milika. I bought her crayons and paper and the child became ecstatic. We spent hours together and hardly noticed it when Martin was not home. And sometimes, when I was away from home she would wait for me to show me what she had drawn that day, jumping up and down, explaining to me about an image that was not the image she was talking about at all. Mother looked particularly different from me, but I loved her just like she did.

As I started to gather more confidence, Joseph encouraged me to use lighter, stronger, more vivid colors, to move away from browns and black. He encouraged me to use the heart more than the mind, that is, to *feel* the image rather than shape the image. That was another challenge, to learn how to shift that gear from the head to the heart.

And so he gradually claimed more and more space in my heart as I went to the big house with trees and dogs as big as wolves. Fearing all the time when he put himself out for me more than Martin did. Joseph let me talk as much as he also talked. He did not tell me that nothing was wrong when everything was wrong. He did not tell me, almost in anger, to stop fretting and settle down. He steered me into new areas, encouraged my efforts. He put challenges before me and then took my hand as I tried to tackle them.

In the beginning, I used to feel nervous, thinking of Martin in Joseph's house, in his presence. But, more and more, as time went on, I relaxed and let my thoughts flow freely, whether they were of Martin or Zima or mother and Godbless. I would think of these people as I mixed colors or painted or framed the canvas ready for work, and I was amazed at how easily my mind released them. And even Martin's image would not stay, it would not hold for long like it used to. Joseph stayed in my thoughts longer, even when he was just yards away. His image held. And I would look at my life, the whole of it to the point where I had reached, and Joseph would be turning and turning around in it like a solid speck of food in a clear glass of water. I would wonder how it had become so, how the heart allowed it to happen even when my mind had not really let go of the love I felt for Martin.

One day, as we were both very involved in the studio, where we spent most of our time together, Joseph said, "I think your mother is a great woman, a woman of steel."

"You have been thinking of her?" I said by way of a question.

"I have been thinking of you," he said. "You have helped me understand things." He went back to the painting, as if it held his hand and asked for his attention. Then after some time, he put the brush away and wiped his hands on the overalls and came to me and said, "You know, for weeks I had been searching. I was not exactly sure of what I was doing, but I thought I was searching for a painting, something to unblock my thinking. I walked the streets, took buses, sat in bars and restaurants, went to the market. I tired, but a voice in me urged me to keep going. When I saw you, something in me stirred and I knew I had to get your attention. I had to know you."

"How does that relate with my mother?" I asked.

"You share the same fate. She brought you up and gave you certain virtues that will serve you well in life. You are fighters, of the spiritual kind. I mean, you would not struggle for money as you would for love or loving. You are the kind that works for justice and not for creature comfort. I was thinking of the emotional energy it took your mother to say she will not go back to her parents, and wondered if I would have done the same. What it has taken to bring the four of you up, alone, instead of getting married to some man who would share that responsibility. And you marry a man you hardly know because he lifts your spirits to great heights instead of opting for a more practical and grounded man."

"It is a difficult option. I would rather have money and stability," I said.

"That is what you think. You would not take money and stability if a drug dealer offered it to you. You would not take money obtained by corrupt means. That is just the way you are. You know, in my years of work, I have done incredibly awful things. I did them all through my career as a diplomat. The salary was good, the position had many benefits and I was very comfortable. After hearing you talk about your life the other day, and seeing how you do not give up on Martin no matter what, I really understood Fe's accusations. Look, I have been a selfish pervert!"

"You are being unfair to yourself. You are feeling remorseful, that is why. You are really a very kind and knowledgeable man," I said, meaning it.

"Lets take a break from these canvases," he said and he led the way into the kitchen. There was a small veranda leading from the kitchen. I stationed myself on one of the chairs as he prepared a snack for both of us. Another thing about Joseph was that there was really no division of work based on sex in his house. He cooked, swept, and washed dishes and clothes, easily, as though it was the most natural thing. It was refreshing to see this in a man.

He came to sit beside me with two plates of sandwiches and said, "I am fifty five and rich. I have enough money to last me the rest of my life and more to go to Fe and Luisa. I have houses I am renting in Europe and shares in some big businesses. I sell my paintings, although what I get from them is peanuts. But then, I am not happy. My wife is gone, my son has almost denounced me. Now, Luisa is like me. Ambitious. She hunts money like nobody's business, but she works hard, very hard. I hate to think where she will end."

"So Justine left you knowing very well how rich you were. That is good. I respect her for that," I said.

He laughed, loudly, throwing his head back. "Oh, yes she knew every thing I owned. She had seen all the legal papers, she knew the bank accounts, everything. Oh, God, you don't know how that has humbled me," he said, looking at me, his eyes filling with tears, but he did not cry.

"Every bit of it. And she is gone. The only thing she accepted from me was the painting: *Parched Earth Needing Water.* I gave it to her as a present," he added. "You remember the pictures of the paintings I showed you," he asked. "*Parched Earth* is one of them. I did it when I learned that Justine had a lover. I became so intensely jealous, oh, I was so jealous. But I desired her more than ever."

He did not speak for some time. He ate quickly, as though he may soon loose the appetite to finish. I went into the kitchen to make instant coffee, which we drank slowly.

I listened.

"I could not have enough of her," he continued, "I had sex with her every time I could - morning, afternoon, evening, night.... I knew she did not want it, that she *hated* it, that she felt *nothing*, but that did not stop me. I was full of vengeance, full of anger. I was overcome with passion, weighed down with it. I called her by every endearing term I knew. I was being consumed. I became restless and sad and thin. I was possessed by a spirit which created such tangles of emotion inside me that I was afraid I was going to maim her...then one day she was gone."

He talked quietly, without the intensity implicit in the words. He drank coffee and shook his head as though he could not believe himself. "God, I was *abusing* her, hating her for not loving me. It has hurt me so much to recognize that I could be such an animal! *Agh*, but I could not forget those letters, those words, I could not exorcise them from my head."

He coughed to clear something in his throat. "Sex had failed to help me, you see. It had no power at all over her. When Justine moved from the bedroom to the guest room, I felt desperate, completely abandoned. I became ghostly thin and my hands started to shake.

Before I killed myself with jealousy I sought out the man. I had to see this man, hold his hand, and hear his voice... I had to and I did.

He was much younger than me, of course. I remember feeling quite surprised that he was so young. I must have looked quite clumsy as I tried to look for words to introduce a subject that was so entangled in the tendons of my nerves that I could hardly talk about it without tearing something in me to pieces. Finally, I managed to introduce myself. He panicked, only briefly, and then a certain resolute curve took life around his mouth. It told me that he would stand his ground.

"Can I help you sir?' he asked me, politely. His voice was rather soft.

I couldn't talk to him, not a word. I think I was mortally afraid of hearing, from his own mouth, that he loved Justine. I could not bear it. Something held my speech and I could not talk. A voice in my head said: shout a few words, scream something, abuse him, spit on him for goodness sake, and then leave.' But, all feeling got trapped in my heart, all the passion for vengeance! I could not hate him, I could not feel anger. I had sought him out thinking that I would beat him up to pulp, that I would kill him even, but I didn't.... Anyway, I came home drenched with self pity."

This one steps on the thorn of the hurt, he pushes the thorn deep into his flesh, I found myself thinking, appreciating the capacity to face all that head on, saluting the mind that was able to know, in the midst of the hurt, that it was doing another wrong. Indeed, two wrongs never righted anything.

"It was my art teacher who prophetically told me that art will save me from madness. She was very right," he said, quietly, sadly.

"I had meant to ask you how you came to paint. I did not know that you went to school to study art," I said. I could not bear to see him reliving more of the pain suffered in the battle with his wife's lover. That was too harsh a position to be in.

He took time to speak again. He sighed, then said, "Oh, yes. I was ambassador in the United States for some years. When I turned forty- six, the government gave me three years before retirement. I suspected there was something cooking, but frankly I was tired. So I went to college to study art, part time. Then after two semesters, I arranged for private classes at home. That was expensive, but I didn't need a certificate, so I didn't have to attach myself to a school. Some positions are a gateway to privilege, you know," he said, smiling "It was thrilling to discover I had a gift for art that I could use to understand life."

I had suspected he would be some important person! I could not have imagined him to have been an ambassador, but I was not going to tell him that. I kept the surprise to myself.

"Why art? Why not something else?"

"Like what?"

"What would ambassadors study? Political science; economics; history perhaps?

He laughed. "In a way you are right. My first degree was in

political science, international relations. I was initially posted to various African countries before I went out into the first world. Before my first posting in Europe, I took two years off and got myself a Master in sociology. I thought I needed sociology in order to understand people and societies. My thesis was titled; 'The Social Dynamics of Labor Organizations in Urban Areas.' Then I was posted in Paris, France. I studied French seriously. I read and write fluently in French. As you can see, this Joseph Selese has been around some."

"But, after studying all those things, why painting?" My teacher's mind was asking for some logic to all this.

"I needed something that I could do without being employed. I did not want to end up with a clean desk without a job description, and looking for a job when you are nearing fifty would be a scandal. And then again, when you work in the diplomatic service for too long, you lose yourself because you are always saying those things that are diplomatically proper, correct. I had always loved and appreciated art, and I thought the longing was deep rooted enough for me to bring out some potential in me. I have been painting for close to seven years. Now, I don't know what I would have done without it."

Suddenly I felt a keen thirst to know the teacher. "Tell me about your art teacher," I asked him. He looked at me, almost pleading for mercy. He was not willing to talk about her, I could see, but he had pulled me into his life already, and I was not going to be a guest at the entrance.

He sighed, saying, "My life is such a mess!"

"Not any worse than mine," I said. "Talk about her," I said again.

"Sabina. That was her name. Her mother was black and her father was white, a bold and incredibly free spirited woman. Her free spirit affected every thing she did and the people she met. We could work and talk about art and culture for a whole day without seeing the passage of time. I was forty- six and she was fifty- four, beautiful, intense and very, very temperamental. I remember thinking, on many occasions that there is no way I could ever marry this one," he said, smiling.

"Why not? She sounds like a solid woman to me."

"I know," he said. It was hard for him to talk about Sabina, I observed. There must be something that still held him to her. Perhaps I was pushing too hard, so I said, "Well, Sabina can wait until next time."

Grudgingly, he said, "I was extremely attracted to her. She knew it but she never indulged in it like most women would do. That intimidated me a bit. She could be so tender, but then she could flare up like fire if I said the wrong word or teased her the wrong way. I could never relax or take anything for granted with Sabina. Yet, there were times I thought I couldn't live without her.

She was a sharp critic who made me want to hide when I had done something she thought was no good, but she was sharp witted too, and energetic and a very accomplished artist. I did not want her to leave after the lessons. I would look for all kinds of excuses to make her stay. I just wanted to be *with* her.

I think that is one woman Justine highly respected. I knew it by the way she paid keen attention to every thing Sabina said. She was Justine's point of reference in serious discussions about art. There were times Sabina would sit with Justine and have tea and talk and laugh. Sometimes she invited Justine to visit her at home. She was single, never married or had children. She lived with her old mother she could not take to old people's home, so she hired a nurse to take care of her when she was away at work.

Sabina invited Justine to the lessons. She however did not pay any attention to her, it was just her way of inviting the other woman's participation. It made me nervous at the beginning before I came to grips with Sabina's indifference to my confused emotions. 'Light is a primary ingredient of art,' Sabina used to say, so she used that principle to keep the studio door open.

After returning home and Justine leaving, when I found myself alone and thought again about Sabina and I, I tend to think that Sabina's spirit possessed me when I was in the studio. I lost my normal self, shed something as I prepared the paints and brushes, the chair where the model would sit, as I prepared the stand and framed the canvas on it. The expectation must have shown in every movement I made. Sabina required me to tell her that I was ready, even as she knew it, and sometimes I behaved like a child waiting for a prize. Maybe that was when Justine knew I was desperately in love with Sabina and she chose to watch it unfold rather than talk about it. But then, even if Justine was pained by it, I could not have seen it at that time.

Justine would come in and watch me paint. She was more interested in me, in my concentration as I brought to life, the parts of Sabina's body on canvas. And when I painted her nude, Justine watched my reactions and responses to Sabina when she changed her pose. Justine looked at the way my mind looked at the model's body, where I tarried a bit longer, the fleeting emotions that washed over my face as I watched Sabina's image almost vibrating with new life in color, on canvas. Then, I would step back and look again at the image - the eyes, the breasts, the stomach and navel, the curve between her legs... and the exaltation showed in my eyes.

Justine and I talked a lot about art. She was good, she had the feel for the elusive and a keen eye for beauty. I always waited for that time when she would give me her opinion about what she had seen. Justine was my *companion*! She already knew, by looking at what I did, that the artist is constantly recreating, translating, interpreting, and overlaying meanings. I thought she liked what I did and what it did to me. She saw that the Sabina I painted was not a photograph of her, and therefore, understood that she was not the subject, that the creation was the subject. I appreciated Justine's interest in my work," he paused. He looked at me, his eyes dreamy. He shook his head.

"Did Justine know you were attracted to Sabina?" I asked.

"I don't know," he said, almost irritably, then, in a more controlled voice, "We talked about Sabina a lot. Her magic affected both of us, really. Only now I see that painting Sabina was singing a love song. Justine must have known, must have felt it, but she never raised it... I miss her feedback. She was so much part of my work in that respect."

"You loved her," I said with sympathy.

He laughed, dryly, shaking his head. "I don't know now. Did I love both women? Did I desire them both? I don't know. I did not, for a long time understand why she had to go and love another man. I associated Justine with *permanence*. Justine was the person who ensured that my life was managed and running smoothly. I did not expect emptiness. I am threatened by emptiness, because it means insecurity, lack of creature comfort, lack of purpose. When she moved around me doing the familiar things- washing, cleaning, cooking, - creating order, a sense of stability, my world felt wholesome.

I realized, after things had gone wrong, that Justine was my companion, but I was not *her* companion. I did not know much of her inner life really. So I did not know when I made her jealous and insecure, I never stopped to notice that she was pained by something I had done or said. She was so controlled, she never flared up like Sabina would. I was more careful with Sabina, and thinking of it later, I was careless with Justine because I felt *safe* with her. I never knew her fears, so I thought she did not have any. I did not ask what she would have wanted most to do other than complementing my work. I wanted my cake, all of it, then I ate it." He shrugged his shoulders.

"As you can see, Sabina gave me a tool to use for my spiritual survival. She taught me a big lesson too: that love between a man and a woman need not be sexual. She taught me that lesson every time I kissed her, pulsating with desire, but never sleeping with her. I do not know how she did it, but she always talked me into waiting, demanding that I be sure first of what I want, whether I was aware of what a sexual relationship would mean to both of us. She must have seen beyond my desire for her and sensed my weakness, my inability to decide between Justine and her. I thank her now for that perception, that solid sense of self which did not feel threatened or mistreated. Anyway, in that process I learned that sharing experiences, talking, learning together and offering friendship and support could also sustain love."

"There is so much I have learned too Joseph," I said, appreciating his humility, thanking him on my part. "There is so much more to learn... Life is about survival, isn't it? What do we do now with the lessons we have learned; do we adapt, like Aunt Mai; rebel like mother or do we run away from ourselves like Martin? What alternatives do we take in order to arrive at that state of just simple happiness?"

He stood up and extended his hand for mine. It was getting dark. I stood up, he put his hand around my waist and steered me from the kitchen veranda where we had sat for a long time, into the sitting room. The smell of his cologne, the softness of his body and its warmth felt familiar and intimate and peaceful.

Before we sat down, he put his head on my shoulder and put both his arms around me, then turning me towards him, said, "I can only thank God for your coming into my life..." He did not say more, he only hugged me for a long time.

I whispered in his ear, "The Wise ones said, we hold miracles in our hands, we are just too short sighted to see." He smiled briefly, becoming serious again, not wanting to let me out his embrace.

"Help me, Doreen," he said, "Give me a bit of your strength. Let us battle this life together," he pleaded.

A thick, hard lump gripped my throat. He looked into my eyes, still pleading, "Please," he whispered, kissing me, holding on to me like a sinking man holds on to a battered, sea beaten raft. Life is about survival, isn't it? The voice of the daemon rose from the depths.

I think everything stood still as I sobered up, as if to find my bearings, my anchor in a strong current. In that very brief instant outside time, the voice rose again; *Its up to you. Its all up to you, Doreen.... to find your own path...*

And later, much later, I heard the chirping of birds outside and somewhere from far away the sound of a car traveling at great speed. Both of us had lost speech. He got up from where we had created space and put on some music, a jazz song whose trumpets filled the silence of the room, blending with the cry of the birds' waking song.